BOOKS BY QUINN AVERY
www.QuinnAvery.com

BEXLEY SQUIRES MYSTERY SERIES

The Dead Girl's Stilettos

The Million Dollar Collar

The Guard's Last Watch

The Skeleton Key's Secrets

The Notebook's Hidden Truths

The Neighbor's Dark Past

STANDALONE ROMANTIC SUSPENSE/THRILLERS

What They Never Said

In Her Father's Shadow

Woman Over the Edge

Deadly Paradise

Lost Girls of Kato

Moscow Mules & Murder

Right Across the Bay

CHILDREN'S BOOKS WRITTEN BY QUINN

Dogs Don't Have Fins

Dogs Don't Have Antlers

The Dead Girl's Stilettos
The Million Dollar Collar
The Guard's Last Watch
The Skeleton Key's Secrets
The Notebook's Hidden Truths
The Neighbor's Dark Past

THE
GUARD'S
LAST
WATCH

A BEXLEY SQUIRES MYSTERY

QUINN AVERY

Cover: Najla Qamber Designs

Photograph by Jenna Loeva

ISBN: 979-8-9895552-6-0

Model: Michael Dicke

www.QuinnAvery.com

PROLOGUE

BAJA CALIFORNIA, MEXICO

OCTOBER 24TH

Brewer Hawkins woke to a tremendous throbbing at the base of his skull. His eyelids felt as if they'd been glued together. A strong, musty stench burned his nostrils, and his stomach churned angrily. He'd had his share of rough nights, especially over the past couple of years, but this felt different somehow.

Finally able to pry his crusty eyelids open, he found himself spread out across a thin-piled carpet, legs askew, jeans and T-shirt covered in a light dusting of dried dirt. His eyes slowly tracked his surroundings. Piles of crumbling brick were the only things inside the small room beyond a dirty, uncovered mattress resting on a box spring. The dust in the air was so thick with dust that he felt a violent sneeze building in his sinuses. He guessed he was either in an abandoned motel or apartment building.

How the hell did he get there, and why did it feel like someone had taken a sledgehammer to his head?

He reached around to touch the source of his pain, muttering obscenities when he discovered an open wound. Congealed blood stuck to his finger-tips. *Had he been in a bar fight again?*

Then, from the corner of his eye, he caught movement.

Blood, dripping off the side of the mattress.

When he clambered to his feet, the thud in his head became a blinding boom.

Stomach violently clenching, he squeezed his eyes closed.

Maybe he was still asleep, and it was only a nightmare. Though he'd never been a religious man, he *prayed* it was a nightmare.

He peered out beneath his heavy eyelids once again until the man's hard features popped back into view. The guy was young, maybe late twenties or early thirties, and lean. Possibly athletic. Hispanic. Dark blue jeans and a light blue button down shirt were accompanied by heavy work boots.

Blood saturated the dirty bedding, spilling down to the floor.

The dark skin between the man's lifeless eyes puckered around a gunshot wound.

Brewer's head throbbed with urgency. His stomach threatened to upheave. He'd seen more than his share of dead bodies, but never in the kind of situation where he had no idea what had happened.

Why was he alone in a room with a dead man?

The room spun as Brewer wiped his mouth on his bare forearm. His gaze trailed along the distance between them, stopping on a Glock .40 caliber. He'd owned several guns since leaving the Coast Guard, but never a Glock.

If anyone were to walk in and find them alone in the room together, likely murder weapon between them, they'd assume the worst. But Brewer was no killer. Not since he was active duty, and protected his country at all costs.

Beyond the corpse, a narrow stream of sunlight streamed through dark, heavy curtains, but it wasn't enough to show a hint of what awaited beyond the four walls of the room.

The last thing he could recall was leaving his repair shop to meet with the president of the Inferno Glory Motorcycle Club. They'd had a few whiskey drinks at a bar near Los Angeles. He had no memories of how he had arrived in that room. When he patted his pockets, he discovered his wallet and cell phone were both missing. Had he been jumped? Why couldn't he remember anything leading up to that moment? He hadn't drank anywhere near enough to black out an entire night.

His gut instinct urged him to dispose of the gun in a body of water somewhere. But he couldn't risk being caught with it in his possession. Removing his dusty T-shirt, he scooped the gun off the carpet to wipe down the grip and slide as best as he could. Then he stood on the pile of bricks and shoved the gun into a crevice. With any luck, no one would think to look up there for a weapon. At least not until he was somewhere far the hell away.

He scanned the room one last time, fearful of any other evidence he'd be leaving behind. As he struggled to get back into his shirt, it occurred to him that he'd likely be leaving strands of hair behind. It was going to take more than luck to get him out of this situation.

He pushed through the room's only door,

revealing a ceramic tiled hallway dim with only a sliver of daylight. Dust particles danced among identical doors lining either side, marked with double numbers. An eerie quietness settles around him, chilling him to the bone.

The sudden urge to bang on each and every door until he found someone to help had him rooted in place, crippled by a rush of paranoia. A place that rundown would only be inhabited by squatters and junkies.

Suddenly an elderly woman appeared at the end of the hallway, the wrinkles on her face deepening as she scowled, speaking rapidly in a foreign tongue. Dark pants and a light blue button down shirt, both of which had seen better days, didn't do anything to reveal her identity. It was unlikely a place like that had a cleaning staff. Dark-skinned, jet black hair pulled back from her face into a low bun, he guessed her to be Hispanic.

"*¡Necesitas irte!*" she yelled, motioning to Brewer with the flicker of her hands. "*¡Ahora!*"

Brewer's head was groggy, and he was still struggling to stand upright. *Spanish*, he realized. *She's speaking Spanish.* He had a good handle on the language from years of confronting smugglers.

"*¿Dónde estoy?*" he blurted.

Where am I?

"*¿Inglés?*" the woman asked with her dark brow raised. When Brewer nodded, the woman's scowl returned with a frantic wave of her hands. "You go. Go!"

"What is this place? Where are we?"

The hardness to the woman's dark eyes softened. She shook her head repeatedly. "*Un mal lugar, señor. Malo.*"

A bad place.

A fight-or-flight response kicked in as Brewer teetered past the woman toward an unmarked door at the end of the hallway. He expected it to lead into another hallway since it wasn't a fire door and didn't say anything about an exit. Shock rippled down his core when he was blasted with sizzling hot air. Worse yet, he was given a view that rendered him immobile.

A Third World village with honest-to-God goats and chickens wandering about unfolded before his eyes.

He nearly choked on the thick air as he took it all in.

He was *in Mexico*.

How in the hell did he not remember entering another country?

Gathering his wits, he swayed toward the nearest shelter within sight. The hut was made out of sticks and grass, held together by mud, and it reeked of human waste. Most importantly, however, it was empty.

He steadied himself against a post, weighing his options. He needed to get to the nearest civilized city. He could locate the U.S. Consulate, but he had no proof of identity.

There was only one number he could recall off the top of his head.

Consequently, that number belonged to the one person Brewer could count on to help him.

PART I

CHAPTER ONE

PAPAYA SPRINGS, CALIFORNIA

OCTOBER 25TH

String instruments accompanied by a piano weaved a complicated melody overhead as Bexley sipped her third glass of Prosecco from a crystal flute. The fine dining restaurant's welcoming atmosphere was a departure from the dives she'd become accustomed to in recent years. It was more her speed if greasy fingers and questionable cooking conditions were involved. Yet it was still easier to acclimate to the dark wallpaper and plush leather chairs among white linens and intricate chandeliers than it was to accept her father's gregarious smile and pleasant demeanor.

A part of her wasn't convinced she hadn't entered some alternate universe the way her sister laughed at the old man's jokes from across the table, carrying on like he hadn't been a cold bastard for a majority of their lives. Just hours before, Bexley had been in shock throughout his entire retirement ceremony as his superiors spoke praises of a man who'd been a solid leader and an excellent adviser to those under his command.

Right before her unbelieving eyes, their father had morphed from a hard-nosed Captain in the Navy who'd continued to neglect his daughters even after their mom's untimely death, to a grandfatherly figure who wanted to fish and travel with his family.

To make matters worse, Bexley constantly felt the questioning gaze of Cineste's boyfriend from across the table. Ever since the former SEAL had come to Bexley's rescue when someone used her as target practice outside their condo, not much got past Alex. The way he was frequently able to see right through Bexley's well-constructed facade was infuriating. The guy worked in construction. Why was his scrutiny so unnerving, like that of a psychotherapist?

Was she still upset over parting ways with her detective boyfriend after they'd essentially started living together? *Of course.* Did nightmares of being thrown into a trunk and accused of murder still snap her out of a deep sleep? *Sometimes.* Could she still hear the cries of incarcerated women from the cells around her late at night? *On occasion.* Did paranoia of being shot at by an unknown enemy still grip her every time she walked through a parking lot? *More often than not.*

Were there times she feared she'd chosen the wrong career path by giving up journalism to become a private investigator?

Abso-freaking-lutely.

But she'd carried on with her life as best as she could, working alongside her mentor, J.J. Stronghold, while attempting to create a semblance of a life that involved more than watching 80s movies in her pajamas with a bottle of wine.

Brewer Hawkins, her once outcast high school classmate turned hunky veteran biker, had played a crucial role in getting her back on her feet after the debacle involving Kappa Kappa Delta. His timing couldn't have come at a better time since her best friend Kiersten had since become heavily occupied with Luke Jacobs, the attorney who'd saved Bexley from bogus attempted murder charges.

Bexley had spent a handful of weekends with

Brewer, sometimes taking in the ocean air on his motorcycle, other times meeting up for a bite to eat. On several occasions, Bexley had gone to his motel on the edge of Los Angeles to drink beers alongside the empty pool.

Though the nature of their relationship remained platonic, and it seemed he preferred dating questionably younger women anyway, she was reluctant to admit just how much she enjoyed every second of his company. Something about the former Coastie's carefree attitude on life struck home. Best of all, he never once lectured her on being careful, or warned her about putting herself in peril. Danger seeped from the man's pores the same way the scent of leather clung to his skin after they'd been on a ride. *And oh, what a lovely scent that was.*

"Bex!" Cineste snapped, eyes narrowing in the candlelight. "Did you hear what Dad said?"

Smoothing the black cocktail dress she'd bought for the occasion against her thighs, Bexley slugged the last gulp of her sparkling wine down before answering. "Sorry, I've been preoccupied by a case." She forced a smile in her father's direction, feeling a ping of relief knowing it was likely the last time she'd see him dressed in uniform. All those medals of honor set against the white tunic were intimidating, to say the least. They even stirred up feelings of guilt for all the contempt she carried against a decorated hero. "What were you saying?"

The old man's brow wrinkled as his eyes, the same green hue as Cineste's and her own, burned with worry. For *her*. It was a phenomena more baffling than Bigfoot sightings. "Maybe you should take some more time off. It's hardly been a month since you were kidnapped and cleared of those absurd charges. Why don't I have a talk with J.J.—"

"That won't be necessary," Bexley insisted. She was mortified by the idea of her father meeting with her boss as if she were a little girl unable to speak her own mind. J.J. knew the only way for Bexley to keep her sanity was to bury herself with work.

Cineste popped a chunk of smoked Gouda into her mouth. "What does Grayson think about you going back to work so soon?"

Looking away from her sister, Bexley's chest pinched with guilt. As far as her family knew, she was still living with Grayson, and they were headed toward the altar. She hadn't told them she was renting a place down the street from Stronghold

Investigations, or that she had been spending a considerable amount of time with another man. She was not about to entertain her family with stories of her love life, or lack thereof.

Snagging her empty glass, Bexley nudged Alex. "Will you grab that waitress behind you? I need a refill."

Alex's deep voice seeped with sarcasm when he answered, "Sure, no problem."

"Are you seeing a psychiatrist?" Bexley's father asked. "Maybe you should look into joining a PTSD group. I've seen it work wonders for brave men who've returned from combat with heads twice as messed up as yours."

Bexley swallowed back a groan. The fact that her absentee father was pretending he knew the first thing about her mental state of mind was absurd. She *was* seeing a psychiatrist, and a majority of their conversations revolved around her lack of parental guidance into adulthood. Until J.J. came into her life, there was virtually no one to give advice when she'd made a mistake, or commend her for her accomplishments.

Around the time she was ready to snag an entire bottle of Prosecco from behind the bar herself, her phone buzzed from inside her handbag draped across the chair. She was giddy with relief for the welcome distraction.

She quickly slipped it out, finding a number starting with +52. Someone was calling her from Mexico. It was unusual, but not outside the realm of normal. Between J.J. and clients, she was accustomed to answering strange calls all hours of the day and night. It was one of the hazards of being a P.I.

"Excuse me," she announced, standing with the cell phone raised in her hand. "I'll just be a minute."

The Captain's back stiffened for a heartbeat, then he grimly nodded his consent. *As if she needed it.* As she hurried away from the table, she caught Cineste's eyes rolling to the ceiling. At least Bexley knew she was a solid 0-2 when it came to the support of her family members.

Pausing beneath a giant tear-drop chandelier outside the restrooms, Bexley finally answered the persistent buzz. "Bexley Squires."

"Bex," a warm, familiar voice rumbled. "It's Brewer."

Picturing his dimpled smirk, her stomach fluttered. She gritted her teeth, deeply annoyed by her Pavlov reaction. "If you're calling to ask for bail money because of a donkey show gone bad, I'm not convinced our friendship has reached that level of depravity."

"I'm calling to ask for a huge favor. I wouldn't put this on you but…there's no one else."

Her heart skipped a beat with the seriousness to his tone. "What do you need?"

"My passport from my motel room…and a ride home…from Tijuana. As soon as humanly possible."

With a heavy sigh, she glanced down the hallway. Though her father wouldn't have thought twice about abandoning them for a work-related matter, she didn't want to throw any further strain into their already tumultuous relationship. "I'm kind of in the middle of something important. Couldn't you ask one of your brothers from the motorcycle club?"

"I'm asking *you* because I need your sleuthing skills. I'll pay you your going rate."

She clutched her phone a little tighter. "Are you in some kind of trouble?"

"Yeah…you could say that."

Eyes closed, she puffed out a little breath. It wasn't in her skill set to turn down a friend in need.

BEXLEY HADN'T MADE THE TWO-PLUS HOUR DRIVE to Tijuana since her senior year in high school. Though the rendezvous hadn't sounded like her cup of tea from the start, Kiersten insisted it was their right of passage to indulge in a wild weekend before graduation. Her best friend had failed to mention a group of their classmates had actually planned the trip, Grayson and his then-girlfriend Amanda Classon included. Bexley was forced to watch her crush drunkenly make out with his future ex-wife for two days straight.

Memories from that weekend came roaring back with painful clarity as Bexley passed the El Chaparral port of entry. Before Grayson got into the tequila that weekend, he'd gone out of his way to show Bexley kindness when everyone else had treated her like a pariah for not wanting to become black-out inebriated. If she knew back then how he'd secretly felt about her, that he reciprocated her feelings, how different would her life be? Would she have stayed in

California, and traded NYU for Papaya Springs College? Would she be the one who married Grayson straight out of college instead of Amanda Classon? Could he have convinced her to start a family by now?

Pushing the wayward thoughts from her head, she focused on the reason she was in Mexico. *Brewer*. She knew very little about the maddeningly handsome biker who came roaring back into her life after ten years. He'd been the quiet kid with questionable hygiene who copied off Bexley's school work. What was so bad about his home life that he'd dropped out of high school at seventeen to join the military? Why did he live in a motel when he ran a successful mechanic shop? Why was he so interested in spending time with Bexley when youthful model-wannabes swarmed him like bees on honey?

As dusk began to fall, she navigated according to Brewer's directions, beyond the highway and onto back roads. What could he have possibly gotten himself into? She hoped it wasn't something criminal. She wasn't exactly up to speed on international laws. Then again, if anything legal came into question, she could always call Luke. He wasn't merely a highly intelligent man who was adored by her best friend. He was quickly becoming one of few included in Bexley's circle of trust.

Once Bexley located the cobalt blue building Brewer had described, she parked her Expedition alongside the curb and held her breath. She'd known better than to bring a handgun into Mexico, but she'd hidden her *stun* gun beneath the passenger's seat. Being far from the heart of the city in a menacing neighborhood, the temptation to retrieve the weapon was strong. Everyone who walked by her vehicle gave her a look that made it clear she wasn't welcome. Even a group of middle school boys walking their bicycles shot deathly scowls that sent chills racing down her limbs.

A full ten minutes passed before she spotted Brewer leaning against the building, lit cigarette pinched between his full lips. She might've mistook him for someone else if it weren't for the distinct illustration of a king's crown inked on the back of his right hand. He wore a pale pink western style shirt and crisp blue jeans that looked extremely out of character on his impressively toned body, yet still made him attractive. His hair was tucked into a baseball cap, pulled low to his honeyed brown eyes that were normally twinkling with mischief. When they found Bexley, they were filled with indisputable worry. Not only that, but he appeared bone-tired.

He flicked the cigarette onto the sidewalk before sliding into the passenger's seat, filling Bexley's vehicle with his unique scent of cigarettes and precariousness. Lips spreading with his signature smirk, he eyed the bodice of her cocktail dress. "You didn't have to get all dolled up for me, sweetheart."

Bexley let out a breath of relief. *At least he was in one piece.* "You said I needed to come here ASAP."

His dark, thick eyebrows rose. "Did I interrupt a hot date?"

She gave him a sharp look, unwilling to buy his nonchalant attitude. "Are you going to tell me what's going on? What are you doing here? Why are *you* dressed like *that?*"

He removed the baseball hat, allowing unruly brown locks to tumble over the shaved sides of his head. "Trying to blend in as a local."

"Ah, so you're delusional. Did your shenanigans down here include a brain injury?"

"Possibly," he deadpanned, glancing out the window. "I might need some stitches once we're stateside."

Her stomach clenched. *What the hell was going on?*

A part of her wanted to hug him. "What happened, Brewer?"

"I'll tell you everything as soon as we're out of this hell-hole." He lifted his chin to the ceiling and leaned back against the headrest. "Just drive." He closed his eyes and added, *"Please."*

Blowing out the long breath she'd planned to use in voicing her objection, Bexley pulled out into the street. Brewer's eyes remained closed, his breath steady. She could practically feel exhaustion rolling off him as she drove.

A few blocks down the street, she came upon a roadblock. The middle school boys on their bikes. The biggest kid in the group stared directly at Bexley, inviting her to a challenge. With a start, she noticed something clutched in his hands. A crowbar.

"Brewer," she pleaded, her throat thick. *"Wake up."*

Brewer shot up in the passenger's seat, one hand clutching the dashboard as he assessed the situation. "Don't suppose they use that for stickball."

"What do I do?"

He glanced over his shoulder. "Throw it in reverse."

Without a second of hesitation, Bexley did just

that. The SUV rocketed backwards, only stopping when Brewer instructed, "Turn here."

With a jerk of the steering wheel, they both leaned over as they rounded the corner. It took several blocks before Bexley's heart resumed a tolerable beat.

She had a sickening feeling the incident was mild compared to what would come next.

CHAPTER TWO

The moment they were cleared to enter back into California, Brewer fell into a deep sleep. There had been a moment in which border patrol scrutinized Brewer and his ID so closely that Bexley was convinced they knew the reason he was in a hurry to leave. Terrified by the idea of being detained in Mexico, she wanted to kiss the Papaya Springs city limits sign when it came into view among the beam of her vehicle's headlights.

She was also eager to shake Brewer awake, and demand he tell her everything. He owed it to her, considering she had dropped everything to save him, alienating her family in the process.

Once she pulled up outside Big Dick's Inn, she finally got her chance. Dozens of red and blue flashing lights cut through the darkness, illuminating the confusion etched in Brewer's groggy expression. The door to his room was propped open by a sheriff's deputy, allowing half a dozen more to enter. For what must've been the hundredth time, Bexley pondered why someone with a successful business chose to live in a dive motel. *Was Brewer running from something?*

"That's a helluva welcoming committee," Bexley commented. "Imagine the fanfare if you had been gone for more than a couple of days."

"It doesn't make sense," Brewer grumbled, running shaking fingers through his hair. "There's no way anyone should know what went down in Mexico. Was anyone around when you entered my room for my passport?"

"I can promise you that aside from getting the key to your room from Big Dick, my presence went otherwise unnoticed. All the curtains facing this side were drawn, and the lot was dark."

"There's no way Big Dick called the cops. He's into some sketchy business on the side and wouldn't want their attention." He turned to Bexley with an accusing stare. "Did you fill your boyfriend in on my situation?"

Bexley's teeth clamped together. "Of course not," she bit out.

Why would he assume she was still with Grayson? Not only did she spend the majority of her free time with Brewer, she hadn't spoken to Grayson in weeks. He'd reached out to her several times, wanting to work things out, but she decided a clean break would be best. Despite their best efforts, their situation would remain static.

Shifting back into drive, she drove on past the motel and threw Brewer a look of annoyance. "I think it's time you tell me what happened in Mexico."

"Problem is, I don't know much." He produced a crumpled pack of Marlboros from his shirt pocket, absentmindedly tapping it against the palm of his hand. "I woke in some shit-hole outside of Tijuana with a gash in the back of my head, no memory of even intending to leave the country. Last I remember is meeting up with Colt Sawyer by L.A. for a drink. Next thing I knew, I was sprawled on the floor of some abandoned building beside a gun… and a man with a bullet hole between his eyes."

Bexley's throat clenched, and her fingers clutched the steering wheel. It was worse than any scenario she had imagined during the long drive down and back. She didn't think Brewer was the type to kill someone in cold blood. Then again, she knew next to nothing about what he'd done, or where he'd been the past decade aside from the Coast Guard.

She paused to let the information sink in. "He was murdered." She wet her lips before glancing his way. "Do you think—"

"*No,*" he snapped, eyebrows scrunching together. "No way. I may be a lot of things, but I'm no murderer."

"Not even in self-defense?"

He tossed the pack of cigarettes onto her dashboard and let out a long breath. "Guess it's always a possibility."

"Did you know the man?"

"Never seen him in my life. He was a local… dressed casual…younger than you and me. In good shape."

"Did you check his pockets for an ID?"

"Didn't really want to get caught disturbing a corpse."

As she turned onto another road, Bexley braced herself for the next question. "Where's the gun now, Brewer?"

"I wiped it down, stashed it in the wall."

It eased her mind somewhat to learn she hadn't helped smuggle a firearm across the border. "Is there any reason there'd be a record of your fingerprints in either Mexico or the US?"

"They might've taken 'em while I was in the service. Can't remember for sure."

"If you *did* fire that gun, there may still be residue on your clothes and hands. We could have it tested…for your state of mind."

Snorting, he caught her gaze. "Want me to march on down to the sheriff's, and willingly submit to a test?"

"They have home kits. J.J. may even know of a way to test for GSR without one."

"Too late. Burned the clothes I was wearing for this getup. Washed my hands several times since."

Bexley's frustration was growing by the second. He wasn't giving her much to work with. "Did anyone see you flee the scene?"

"Just some elderly woman who spoke limited English. When I asked her where I was, she just responded with, 'a bad place' and told me to go. I walked for several hours, following backroads north. I wasn't completely convinced it was the right direction, so I went in search of a main road…hitched a ride with a truck full of factory workers. The guys I sat next to kept to themselves and didn't acknowledge my presence. By that time, we were only a half hour or so out of Tijuana."

"Do you have any reason to think someone would try to hurt you?"

"Besides a handful of women pissed off because I don't do relationships?"

She glanced his way to find him smirking. Normally she found that playful look of his enduring, but in that moment, it was testing her patience. "Brewer, if there's something you aren't telling me that could possibly connect you to that man, now's the time."

With a low grunt, he retrieved the pack of Marlboros. "I'm not gonna lie to you, Squires. I've done some crooked shit over the years, but never anything that would physically harm someone. I guarantee I didn't have anything to do with that man's death. I'm well aware my temper can be a problem, but I'd never take things that far."

"Have you asked Colt Sawyer if he knows what happened that night?"

"Someone took my phone along with my wallet. I don't know the guy's number off-hand. I'd pay a visit to the clubhouse, but that doesn't seem like a wise move, all things considered." He popped a cigarette between his lips. "Hate to ask you for another favor, but would you mind dropping me somewhere near the beach? I know of a few places where the cops wouldn't come looking."

Bexley tapped her fingertips against the steering wheel. "Have you mentioned my name to anyone recently? Maybe told someone at the motel, or club, or your shop that we've been meeting up?"

With a chuckle, he rubbed at his chin. "Seems an odd time to ask if we're a 'thing'. Are you asking me out?"

Her cheeks burned hot as she shook her head. Is that the direction he assumed they were headed? "If you haven't, you can stay at my place until this blows over, or at least until we know more." There was a slight chance someone had spotted them together in recent weeks, but her experiences led her to believe her notoriety hadn't spread beyond Papaya Springs. And the way Brewer stayed to himself, she didn't think he was well-known. "It wouldn't be a problem...I have a spare room."

Glancing over his shoulder, Brewer's lips twisted with another teasing smirk. "Your boyfriend seemed pretty convinced I'm the scum of the earth. Sure he'll allow a sleepover with a wanted criminal?"

A flame of anger ignited in Bexley. "Grayson and I have been done for *weeks*. Regardless, it still wouldn't have been his decision. And we don't have any idea why the sheriff is raiding your place. Maybe something unrelated to your situation went down while you were gone. It's not like the other occupants at Big Dick's are model citizens. A number of things could've happened."

He quirked one eyebrow. "You ditched the suit? I'm impressed, Squires."

Did he even hear what she had said about the sheriff? She shook his comment off with a dismissive flick of her hand. "I'm gonna find a way to get you out of this mess, Brewer." Fatigue weighed heavily on her shoulders as she veered back toward the interstate. "Just not tonight."

BEXLEY SNUCK OUT EARLY THE NEXT MORNING while Brewer was still asleep in the guest bedroom. She'd cleaned the wound on his head the night before, and was worried it was deep enough for medical attention. At Brewer's insistence, however, she'd merely applied super glue to keep it closed. She left a note beside a burner phone and a leftover bagel from breakfast the day before, telling him to check his wound for signs of infection, and to avoid contact with anyone. She also left her direct number at the office, instructing him to call as soon as he was awake.

Once her mind began processing his story, she'd barely caught any sleep. It'd be difficult to conduct a proper investigation without returning to the scene of the crime. Even if Brewer remembered how to get there, she wasn't going to risk putting him in the hands of the *Federales*. The idea that the local authorities may already be onto his situation made her uneasy, especially considering her past experiences with Sheriff Blair. He wasn't the kind of man to be trusted. But the idea that the sheriff may be after Brewer for something else was even more unsettling.

The moment Bexley stepped foot inside the familiar surroundings of Stronghold Investigations, she was alerted to her boss's presence with the sounds of a barking cough from behind his closed office door. Although J.J. claimed to have humored her several weeks ago by going to see a doctor, she highly doubted they'd written off his condition as a mere cold. She feared there was something serious behind that smoker's cough, and J.J. had become more important to her than she could put into words.

As it was their secretary's day off, Bexley started a pot of coffee before firing up her laptop and checking her emails. The first one to catch her eye was from Luke Jacobs with a subject line of 'Pending Litigation'. Bexley's heart dropped as she read the contents. A trial had been set for the girls involved in the Kappa Kappa Delta hazing incidents, but the special district attorney had officially declined to press charges related to Bexley's kidnapping. They didn't believe they had enough evidence against any one person specifically to form a solid case.

Bexley clicked on the video attachment Luke included in his email. The Papaya Springs mayor stood with a triumphant smile on the courthouse steps, District Attorney Jenkins at his side. With a chill, Bexley was reminded of the time the two men stood outside the sorority house and warned her to back off with her investigation into a pledge who nearly died from alcohol poisoning.

"The fine citizens of Papaya Springs can once again rest easily," Mayor Hoffman belted out, hands raised at his sides like a preacher on his pulpit. "Despite slanderous allegations made by a confused young woman affiliated with Kappa Kappa Delta, the justice system has proven I'm an innocent man. With my re-election on the horizon, I fear this won't be the last attempt made by my opponents to smear my name. I can assure you, however, that any further accusations will be thwarted the moment that they're made, and you can vote for my second term with confidence."

A bevy of emotions rose from the pit of Bexley's stomach. They may have removed District Attorney Jenkins from the case because of his daughter's involvement in the sorority, but someone had clearly bribed his successor into looking the other way. They'd come after Bexley again. She was sure of it. Mayor Hoffman and DA Jenkins weren't going to stand back and allow her to continue her expose of their beloved residents and their corrupt ways. While she was terrified by the lengths they may go to next, a part of her willed them to try.

"I get knocked down, but I get up again," she muttered aloud.

"You say something?" J.J. drawled from her doorway, steaming cup of coffee in hand.

Bexley cleared the thickness from her throat and shut her laptop. "Just warming my pipes for the day with a little Chumbawamba."

The old man's features tightened with a frown. "A little *what*?"

For the first time since she'd met him, his white hair wasn't its usual fluffy texture. It wasn't only limp, but it appeared to be thinning. The way his clothes hung on his frame, it would seem he had recently lost weight too. Was it possible he'd aged that much in the short amount of time they'd known each other?

"You feeling alright, old-timer?" Bexley asked, clasping her hands together and setting her elbows on the desk. "I know you've been around since before electricity was invented, so it's understandable if you're a little worn down, but you look exceptionally exhausted."

He tugged at the small silver hoop in his left ear. "I feel just fine, darlin', so you can wipe that worried look off your face."

"Either you're lying, or you've adopted a pet seal. I heard you when I came in."

His head hung a little as he took the chair on the other side of the desk and set the cup of coffee within her reach. From the somber look on his face, Bexley already knew what he was about to say would be grim.

"I've been meanin' to talk to you about something." He settled back in the chair, arm slung over one side, gaze settling on the floor. "As the saying goes, I'm not getting any younger. Since I won't be around forever, I need to get my affairs in order—including this place." He paused, lifting his chin to hold her concerned stare. Bexley swore she saw moisture building in his grayish-blue eyes. "Bein' that I don't have any next of kin, I was thinkin' I'd pass the business along to you."

Tears stung behind her own eyes. The gesture meant more to her than he would ever know, but she didn't like the direction of his thoughts. "What aren't you telling me, J.J.?"

"Everything's fine…no need to worry. I'm not checking out just yet." He rubbed at his chin thoughtfully. "But the docs think I may have a moderate case of COPD—a lung disease. Makes it hard to breathe is all."

"Is it," she stopped to swallow the lump in her throat, "fatal?"

"Just means I gotta quit smokin'. Either way, I'm gettin' kinda old to be chasin' criminals around Papaya Springs." He bent forward with a warm smile. "What d'ya say, darlin'? It'd give me peace of mind to know you're up for taking over the business."

"It'd be my honor," she croaked out.

"You're a good, smart woman with a bright future. Wouldn't want anyone else operatin' under my name." With a wink, he leaned back in the chair. "What're you doin' here so early on a Monday mornin' anyway? Shouldn't you be recoverin' from a hot date over the weekend?"

Wiping at her damp eyes, she openly laughed at his attempt to pry into her personal life. He was one of few who knew her and Grayson had called it quits, yet he had graciously never pressured her into a conversation about how it made her feel. Still, she wasn't surprised he wanted to know if she had moved on. The man's concern for her was far deeper than her own father's.

"I agreed to take on a new client last night whose innocence is under question. I'd rather not get into the details until I know more."

"Alright. What d'ya need from me?"

She eyed the pen from Cineste with "*Be a quick-wit*" embossed in gold. For whatever reason, the damn thing always inspired her in some way. "Do you know a way a person could search for death records in Mexico without leaving a digital footprint?"

J.J.'s eyes burned with disapproval. "This new client of yours involved with the *Federales*?"

"Not at this point." *At least she didn't believe so.*

"Sure you wanna take this one on? Murders that take place in Mexico never end well, whether or not a person's guilty."

"He's a good friend of mine, J.J. I don't believe he's capable of killing anyone. At least not without good reason."

Letting out a raspy sigh, he lifted his shoulders. "A buddy of mine has a granddaughter who's a first-rate hacker…graduated from MIT with honors. I've used her a couple'a times. She's a little green behind the years and a little quirky, but she knows her stuff. I'll send you her contact info."

"Thank you, J.J." She wet her lips. "For everything."

Bexley didn't trust herself to say anything more without breaking down. She couldn't bear the thought of losing another person she loved.

CHAPTER THREE

J.J. hadn't exaggerated when he mentioned the hacker was "quirky." Ashton Casey was a petite redhead—the scarlet shade one gets from a bottle—with plush lips and a button nose, a dozen piercings between her ears, and a colorful *Star Wars* themed sleeve tattoo running up one arm. She wore torn blue jeans paired with a sleeveless t-shirt the same striking emerald tone as her eyes, bright red lipstick, thick crimson locks in a haphazard bun. Bexley decided on first sight the girl was cute in an in-your-face kind of way.

Just twenty minutes after their phone conversation, she breezed into Bexley's office with a laptop tucked under her arm and a megawatt smile.

"What up, Buttercup?" Ashton sang, grabbing a

chair meant for clients and dragging it around to Bexley's side. The girl then proceeded to set her top-of the line computer on the desk, and open the screen.

"I'm gonna take a wild guess, and say that you're Ashton." Bexley quirked a brow. "Can I get you anything? Perhaps your name engraved on the door?"

"Call me Red. Everyone else does…for obvious reasons." Ashton snapped her gum and rolled her eyes to the ceiling before her focus honed in on her laptop. "This could take a minute. I haven't had time to clean the hard drive in awhile."

The usually stuffy room became animated with the sounds of Red humming a whimsical tune as her computer whirled to life. Bexley was worried she'd choke on the air that was all at once thick with the girl's overpowering lavender perfume and watermelon bubble gum.

Red glanced Bexley's way. "You been doin' this P.I. gig long?"

"I'm still a bit green behind the ears. What about you?"

"I started hacking before I learned to ride a bike, which really pissed my dad off, considering he's a profiler for the FBI." She snapped her gum while squinting at her computer screen. "Okay, I'm ready. What's this super-secret thing you want me to search?"

Bexley hesitated. The girl could pass for a seventeen-year-old. "You understand you're doing this as a sub-contractor to Stronghold Investigations, therefore bound by confidentiality?"

"Of course. You're not my first client, sweets. Definitely not as high profile, either." *Gum snap.* "Your secrets are safely sealed behind these cherry lips." She puckered said lips and made a smacking sound. "My other gig—doing IT for introverts who only shop online—is as painful as watching a Stormtrooper try to hit a moving target. I'm desperate for intellectual stimulation. Lay it on me, boss-lady."

"Let's start with a list of all arrest warrants issued in the past forty-eight hours out of Currie County."

Red's stubby fingernails, painted a glittery silver, flew across the keyboard while her eyes stayed glued to the screen. "That's an easy one. There were only two: one for a Richard Davis Boon, and one for a Pamela Lee Rattai. Oooh, Pam was a *naughty* girl. Indecent exposure and lewd acts. Sounds like a wild night."

"That's it? No other names came up?"

"Just our friends Dick and Pam."

Bexley tapped her index finger against her lips. If the sheriff wasn't officially searching for Brewer, why would they have raided his motel room? Could there have been a crime committed in his absence? "What about search warrants?"

Red resumed humming for several minutes as she typed. Then, "None issued in that time frame."

That in itself was a red flag. If Sheriff Blair was conducting a search under the table, it meant someone powerful in the community was after Brewer. Fear rendered her numb with a sudden thought. She wasn't going to lie to herself. Brewer had become someone of great importance to her, and it may have been obvious to anyone with two eyes. Including her enemies. What if the Mayor and DA were having Bexley followed? What if they planned to get back at her by hurting those she cared about? What if they knew Brewer was at her apartment?

"What's next, boss-lady?" Red asked, snapping her gum.

Shaking the paranoia away, Bexley cleared her throat. "Let's do a search for death records within a hundred mile radius of Tijuana that would've occurred on or around Saturday night. I'm looking for a Hispanic male between sixteen and thirty-five."

"Most women prefer their potential suitors to be living, but whatever floats your boat," she sniggered. "I'm not here to judge."

Despite her best efforts to remain professional, Bexley's shoulders shook with a silent giggle. She already liked this kid. Although she tried to follow what Red was doing, there must've been a privacy filter over the screen since it appeared black. "You're positive this search can't be traced back to this location?"

"Please. I'd be locked in Club Fed, playing tennis with politicians for the rest of my life if Uncle Sam knew even a smidgen of my shenanigans. The FBI has been begging me to come work for them ever since I was accepted to MIT. I told my dad to have me committed if I ever agreed to such a thing. I saw firsthand what working for the government can do to a marriage. No thank you." Red's fingers stopped, and she let out a low whistle. "Seems Tijuana had a busy weekend. Do you know a cause of death?"

"Gunshot, although there could've been more involved."

Red's fingers danced some more. "We have an Alejandro García, born in 1998; a Martín López, born in 1991; and a Nicolás González, born in 1993. All from gunshot wounds, all within a hundred mile radius of Tijuana."

Bexley tilted her head, wishing she could see the screen. "Do the records include pictures?"

"No, but with my Jedi tricks, I can get you some in a flash."

As Red's magic fingers resumed their work, Bexley's cell phone rang with a call from an unknown number. Suspecting it to be the burner she'd given Brewer, she snatched it off her desk and stood. "I'd appreciate any information you can dig up regarding each of those three men. I'll be back in a minute." Then she slipped into the hallway, closing the door to her office before answering, "Bexley Squires."

Brewer's deep, groggy voice answered, "Before I opened my eyes this morning, I thought you coming to my rescue was only a dream. A really, really *good* dream."

A flush spread across Bexley's neck. "You haven't been officially rescued yet, but I'm working on it. So far I have good news. By tonight, I should have pictures of men from that area of Mexico who died over the weekend. I realize it could be a long-shot, but maybe you'll recognize one. And Currie County hasn't a warrant of any kind for you within the past forty-eight hours. Neither to search your property, nor for your arrest."

"Does that mean I can split? It's pretty lonely here, and I'm itchin' for a smoke."

"It *means* you need to stay put and be aware of your surroundings at all times. The sheriff may not have gone through the proper channels to search your place for a number of reasons, none being in your favor." Bexley turned in the direction of J.J.'s closed door and lowered her voice. She never knew when the old man was listening. "My Glock is in the nightstand drawer beside my bed…passcode eight-six-seven-five. Keep it close, just in case."

"The cunning Bexley Squires chases after bad guys for a living, and leaves her weapon at home?"

Her lips pinched together. She wasn't in the mood for a Grayson-style lecture, and she definitely wasn't going to disclose the fact that guns made her uneasy.

Brewer surprised her with a chuckle. "Who would've thunk it? You're even more badass than I thought, Squires."

"You can smoke inside," she grumbled, even

though she'd likely lose her deposit. "Just do it by a cracked window. And keep the curtains drawn. You wouldn't be lonely if they hauled you off to jail—especially once they throw me in along with you."

"I'm sorry to put you through this," he said, his deep voice becoming grave. "I promise to make it up to you, Bex. And I don't just mean money-wise. I appreciate that you're putting everything on the line to help me. I know you can't afford to get caught harboring a criminal. Just say the word, and I'm outta here. I understand if it gets to be too much. I wouldn't be able to live with myself if anything were to happen to you."

Bexley's breath hitched. They were the most thoughtful words she'd heard him utter. She'd always suspected there was more to her old friend beneath the tough persona and constant jokes, and she was delighted to catch a glimpse. But was she reading too much into what he was saying?

"That's the second time you've called yourself a criminal," she scolded. "Is there something you aren't telling me?"

"We'll talk when you get home."

Home. She found it odd that the sudden notion of sharing her apartment with Brewer on a more permanent basis didn't scare her. In fact, she kind of liked it. But was it because she felt sorry for her old friend who lived out of a seedy motel, or was it because she enjoyed his company more than she wanted to admit?

She looked down at her phone to discover Brewer had ended the call. Jarred by the idea of inviting him to live with her, she'd overlooked the smooth way he had avoided her question. Was he hiding something?

Determined to uncover more pieces to the puzzle, she marched back into her office. Red presented her with a large stack of printer paper. "You should consider upgrading your office equipment. Your printer is slower than my grandma shuffling off to bingo."

"Are you any good at finding personal cell phone numbers?"

"Are Luke and Leia twins despite that creepy kiss?" When Bexley merely stared back, confused, Red clicked her tongue. "That means without a doubt. Lay it on me, sister. Who you wanna call?"

"Colt Sawyer, the president of Inferno Glory Motorcycle Club."

"You've got strange taste in men, lady, but I dig it. Give me a few minutes, and I'll have your Prince Charming's digits."

Bexley felt a small rush of relief. With any luck, she'd have a chance to talk to the one person who may have an idea of how Brewer ended up in Mexico.

BEXLEY'S REQUEST TO MEET WITH COLT SAWYER was granted as soon as she'd mentioned it was regarding the fate of someone in his club. Once she followed his directions to a bar near L.A. named "Mikey's," she wasn't surprised to find a row of Harley Davidsons parked in front of the small establishment—some of which were identical to Brewer's model.

The first time she had met Colt, the sultry club president, she was undercover in search of a biker —one who turned out to be Brewer. Colt mentioned their club had made their share of enemies, and he'd been wary of her presence on their turf. She figured he wouldn't come to their meeting alone, and almost asked J.J. to tag along. But instead she had left a note on her desk, telling J.J. where to come looking if he didn't hear from her by the end of the day.

Inside the dive bar, the smell of cheap beer and

sounds of a woman wailing a twangy tune over-whelmed Bexley's senses. Despite all the motorcy-cles outside, the place was nearly empty. The only other patrons consisted of a middle-aged couple cuddling in a booth toward the back. Her first intu-ition made her believe the bikers had too much to drink the night before, and hitched a ride home. Her second guess, that they were waiting to make an ambush, left her feeling uneasy. Maybe Grayson was right. Maybe she had a death wish.

Bexley only made it a few steps when a hand-some man behind the bar with a hooked nose sent her a blindingly crooked smile. "Hey there, beauti-ful," he called out, blueish-green eyes sparkling with mischief. "What can I get you?"

Bexley's eyes traveled to the name embroidered on his shirt. "Hey there, Mikey. I'm assuming this is your bar?"

He winked. "Sure is. What brings you here?"

"Colt Sawyer."

Mikey nodded among a grin. "He's been expecting you. He stepped out back for a smoke. I'll let them know you're here."

Rattled by the idea of an entire gang coming out to meet her, she rushed up to a bar stool and called after the man right as he turned his back. "Can you get me a shot first? Something *strong*."

The man chuckled. "Sure thing." He set a shot glass between them, and made a show of pouring something dark. "This will put hair on your chest." He nudged the glass in Bexley's direction, eagerly watching her gulp it down.

Bexley had obviously never chugged gasoline, but she guessed the experience wouldn't be much different. Warmth and courage seared her stomach as she fished a ten out of her handbag. "Thanks. I needed that."

"I get the feeling you don't have much experience with MC culture, so I'm gonna give you a little advice: you don't have any reason to be nervous. Colt's a good man. If you don't mess with his family, there's nothing to worry about."

He disappeared for a few tension-wrought minutes, and reappeared with Colt Sawyer a step behind. The beautiful brunette Colt had been cozied up to the night Bexley visited their clubhouse was at his side, followed by a giant man sporting long hair and a full beard. Bexley faintly remembered seeing the attractive man glued to another female biker's side that same night. The three of them were stunning as a trio, clad in variations of leather and denim, oozing sex appeal. Bexley caught herself reacting in a way that felt a lot like swooning.

Colt tucked a strand of wavy brown hair behind his ear, exposing his chiseled jaw. As the brunette watched on with a guard-dog style stare, Colt regarded Bexley with a tilted head. "Why do I get the feelin' we've met before?"

"We have…at your clubhouse." Bexley twisted her fingers together at her waist, hoping her cheeks weren't as red as they felt. "Only I was undercover, hoping to find someone to lead me to the young woman I'd supposedly murdered."

Crossing his thick arms over his broad chest, Colt laughed. "How'd that turn out for ya?"

"She was hooking up with Brewer Hawkins… and very much alive, I might add." She extended her hand between them. "Bexley Squires. I'm a private investigator. I was hired by Brewer to help him out of a delicate situation."

Shaking her hand, Colt nodded. "I figured somethin' was up, considerin' his bike has been here since the other night. This is my wife Harley, and my brother, Ranger. Let's have us a seat." He caught Mikey's attention. "Bring us a round of Jameson—get one for yourself too."

Mikey lifted his chin high before Colt led them to a long table located far from the only other occupants. Harley finally relaxed when she settled at her husband's side.

"Is Brewer alright?" Colt asked. "A couple of sheriff's deputies stopped by my clubhouse, askin' if I knew where they could find 'im."

Bexley's entire body tensed. "Did they say why?"

"They didn't seem too keen on sharin' details," Ranger commented in a deep, barking tone. "Can't say I'd trust a single one of 'em."

Bexley swung her gaze back on Colt. "He's having a hard time remembering the events of last Friday after the two of you got together. Can you walk me through that night?"

"Met 'im here…around seven," he said. "He only had a few drinks—no more than usual. Yet somehow he was a mess, slurrin' his words and wobblin' on his feet. Harley had planned to come give 'im a ride home once he was ready to head out."

Interesting, Bexley thought. *It almost sounded as if Brewer had been drugged.* "How long was he here? Did you see him leave?"

"He'd been flirtin' all night with a fiery little

thing…wouldn't leave 'im alone from the moment he walked through the door." The side of Colt's mouth lifted with a smirk. "They eventually started makin' out…got real hot and heavy. Then she suggested they go out back…told me he'd return in a few. When he didn't show, I figured she'd taken 'im to her place for the night."

Bexley loathed the surge of red-hot jealousy that overshadowed every other emotional response to the story. "Did you catch this woman's name?" she asked. "Had anyone seen her around here before?"

The biker shrugged. "Don't think she said."

Mikey arrived with their drinks just then. "You ever seen that woman Brewer hooked up with on Friday night?" Colt asked.

Mikey looked up at the ceiling, scratching his head. "Not that I remember."

Bexley waited until Mikey headed back to the bar to ask, "Why did you meet with him that night, Colt?"

"He wanted to explain why he'd left the club," he said. "He was hopin' I'd know a way to help 'im out of a problem. Guessin' by the way law enforcement seems to want a piece of 'im, things have gotten worse."

Brewer left the club? Why hadn't he mentioned that to Bexley? He also hadn't explained why he met with Colt that night. She asked him straight out if there was anything he needed to share. Hearing that he came to Colt for help with something annoyed her more than she could handle.

He already knew he was in trouble long before the incident in Mexico.

"What *problem* are you referring to?" she asked.

Colt's beautiful sky-blue eyes cut to Ranger, then fell back on Bexley. "If you don't know, darlin', then I've already said too much. I think maybe it's time for you to leave."

Bexley agreed. Standing, she tossed a business card on the table. "If you remember any other important details about that night, give me a call."

CHAPTER FOUR

Because of the note she'd left in her office, Bexley knew she had to stop by to check in with J.J. before confronting Brewer. The bossman was out, likely for lunch, so she scrawled a note on his desk before grabbing the information Red had printed on the deceased men. When she started for the front door, she came face-to-face with Kiersten.

"Sexy Bexley!" her friend squeaked, flinging her arms around Bexley's neck. "I haven't seen you in forever!"

Bexley patted Kiersten's back before maneuvering away. "That's because you're too busy playing tonsil hockey with my attorney."

Kiersten crossed her arms over her pale blue

designer suit jacket, and snorted. "What is this, junior high? I thought you liked Luke."

Hesitating, Bexley assessed her blonde fashionista friend. She didn't think she'd ever seen Kiersten *not* perfectly made up, with a single hair out of place. Yet that day, something was amiss. The foundation under Kiersten's eyes was caked on, her dress capris weren't crisply ironed, and her golden locks spilled from the kind of lazy bun Bexley wore to the gym.

"Luke's a good guy," Bexley conceded. *You just haven't been around when I needed you,* she thought to herself. She added with caution, "If you're *happy* with him, I'm happy."

Kiersten's smile wavered. "Have you and Grayson tried working things out?"

Mentally bracing herself, Bexley willed her eyeballs not to roll. "As much as I'd love to catch up with you, I was just on my way out for lunch."

"Perfect!" Kiersten hooked her arm through Bexley's. "I'm starving, and there's a new little vegan cafe down on the boardwalk I've been dying to try. Come on, it'll be my treat. I'll even drive."

Bexley gave in, knowing she'd hurt her friend's feelings if she refused. Besides, she wanted to make sure there wasn't more in Kiersten's seemingly perfect life that was amiss beyond her appearance.

As soon as she was seated in the soft passenger seat of Kiersten's new Lexus, she sent a text to the burner phone.

Was planning to bring you lunch. Plans changed. Should be a box of mac & cheese in the pantry. I'll be there as soon as I can.

Remembering Colt's story about the woman at the bar, Bexley wanted to chuck her phone out the window. She couldn't wait to hear Brewer's reasoning as to why he wanted to meet the club president on Friday night, and why he hadn't mentioned it sooner.

On the short drive to the beach, Kiersten chatted happily about her recent dates with Luke. The conversation was one-sided, with Bexley merely humming and uttering an occasional, "wow" in response. The way Kiersten carried on, almost to herself, Bexley suspected her friend was nervous. Her intuition was confirmed as soon as they were seated at a table on the cafe's patio, and Kiersten's cheery demeanor vanished. Face ashen, she reached out to place her hand over Bexley's.

"Bex, I have a confession to make. I asked you to lunch because I need your help."

A protective feeling seized Bexley's insides. "Is this about Luke? Because if he's done something to you, I'll cut his—"

"Oh my god, no!" Kiersten released a little nervous giggle and withdrew her hand. "Luke's *amazing*…treats me like a queen. He's actually the one who suggested I come to you."

"In that case, how can I be of service, your highness?"

"Something happened at work. Something I can't wrap my head around. And if my boss finds out, I'll be fired *and* ostracized from the industry." With a trembling hand, she lifted her water for a delicate sip before setting the glass down again. "I was in charge of a fashion show over the weekend —the biggest Papaya Springs has ever seen. I was entrusted with dozens of designs from some of the biggest names in the industry, and rare pieces from world-renowned jewelers. We're talking millions of dollars' worth of inventory. I'd hired fifty security guards to cover the event. There were two posted at every exit, and ten assigned to watch over the models and inventory." Her eyes glistened with tears. "I didn't take the responsibility given to me lightly."

"I can't imagine you would," Bexley said, nodding. Guilt for assuming Kiersten was ignoring her because of Luke scratched at her conscience. She wished she'd known her friend was taking on such a large project.

"The show itself went smoothly for the most part—nothing a safety pin and body tape couldn't fix anyway. We were given a *five minute* standing ovation. It was insane."

"I wish you would've told me about the show. I would've been there in a heartbeat."

Kiersten laughed. "I know it's not really your kind of thing." She wiped at a fallen tear. "Anyway, it wasn't until after the models had left and I was helping security pack up the inventory when I realized there was something off about one of the most valuable pair of earrings. They were too flawless. They'd been swapped out for the originals at some point while they were in my custody. They were designed by Shantel de Ellis in the forties. I know that name probably doesn't mean much to you, but they featured four hundred thousand dollars in emeralds. What I found in the box was an expertly constructed knock-off."

Bexley uttered a low whistle. "With that much on the line, I completely understand your concern. Sounds like someone planned the heist ahead of time. How far in advance did you know you were getting those specific earrings?"

"Several weeks."

"Other than you and the jeweler, who knew about them?"

"The models involved, and everyone on my design team," Kiersten explained as more tears fell. "They were posted on the visual board for the past week and a half. The model who wore them the night of the show rehearsed with them two nights prior."

"Have you interviewed each of the models and your design team? What about your security guards? Have you asked to review the surveillance footage from the venue?"

"The venue said it's going to take some time to burn the feed to a CD since the head of their security is the only one who knows how to properly do it, and he's out of the office until tomorrow. I've been calling people non-stop since Saturday night. Everyone I spoke with doesn't remember seeing anything unusual. Simone, the model who wore the earrings, broke down in tears, said I could give her a polygraph and whatever else was necessary to prove her innocence. She swears she had nothing to do with their disappearance. She claims she handed them off to a security guard, and watched him place them inside the jeweler's box. Thing is, I've worked with that girl for several years. Simone's a sweetheart. She wouldn't hurt a fly."

Bexley hoped to meet with this *Simone* to see for herself if she was as innocent as Kiersten believed. She'd been duped enough times that she'd started to understand everyone involved was a suspect. "What did that security guard have to say?"

"He swears he secured the earrings the way I'd instructed, and said they looked exactly the same as they had when he handed them to Simone. I called his employer, and they had nothing but praise for him…said he was coming up on twenty years with them."

"Did anyone else have access to that area? Building personnel? Caterers? Photographers?"

"There were at least a hundred people cleared for backstage access. I've only managed to inter-view, like, thirty so far." She sniffled, swiping the back of her hand over her wet cheeks. "At first I tried to keep what happened a secret from Luke, but he figured it out on his own and said this was too monumental for me to handle on my own. He told me I either needed to contact you or the police. I chose you for obvious reasons. I called in sick to work this morning, and was able to convince the Shantel de Ellis representative that their earrings will be returned by the end of the day." She let out a small, muffled sob. "Bex, no one in the business will ever trust me again! My career is over!"

Bexley reached out to squeeze Kiersten's trembling hands. "Not if I can get to the bottom of this. I'll come up with a way to stall their return to the jeweler. I'm going to need you to give me the counterfeit earrings, and the names of everyone given backstage clearance. In the meantime, I'll meet with Simone and the security guard in person to see if there's anything important they failed to mention."

SIMONE PAXTON'S 4-STORY APARTMENT COMPLEX was located on the east side where the service industry workers resided. Housing was more affordable, although still not inexpensive by any means, and the crime rate was low. Lawns were uniformly mowed, bushes trimmed, houses well-maintained, and basketball hoops adorned every third garage.

In most communities, it would've been considered a middle class neighborhood. To the wealthy residents of Papaya Springs, anyone who lived on the east side was regarded as being hardly one step above cockroaches.

As soon as Bexley rang the doorbell to unit 105, she was greeted by the annoying yip of a small dog. A moment later, she heard a man yell, "Shut the hell up, stupid mutt! Go find your mom!"

There was a high-pitched squeal, then the door swung open. A caucasian man in his mid-twenties with a surfer-style shag haircut and bloodshot green eyes greeted Bexley, pale lips twisted in a sly grin. A dry wet-suit hung from his waist, showcasing a decently toned chest featuring a tribal tattoo. Bracing a flexed bicep against the doorframe, he flicked his head, causing his bronzed bangs to feather out across his forehead. "What can I do you for, sweetheart?"

"Oh you've got to be kidding," Bexley muttered under her breath. She straightened her spine and forced a passable smile. "Hello, *Travis*. Remember me?"

The cook from La Belle tilted his head, eyes wide. "Bruh! You're that hot lady that came around the restaurant, askin' about some dog collar! You here to take me up on that date?"

Bexley's artificial smile suddenly felt cemented in place. "Does Simone Paxton live here, or have I merely entered some bizarre universe in which nightmares come to life?"

"Yeah, this is her place." His eyebrows lowered with a suspicious stare. "What do you want with my sister?"

What were the chances that one of Kiersten's coveted models was the sister of a stoner chef? Bexley made a mental note to check Travis's criminal background. While she highly doubted Travis could be the mastermind behind an elaborate heist, he still could have some level of involvement. "I just need to ask her a few questions. Is she here?"

"Yeah hold on." He turned to shout over his shoulder, "Simone, *dude*, get your ass out here! Some bangin' hot chick wants you!"

"Classy as always, Travis," Bexley commented dryly.

After yelling her name again, a tall, gangly young woman came stumbling in behind him in a leopard print cami pajama shorts set, black hair askew beneath a pink eye mask, eyelids nearly squinted shut against the sunlight streaming through the doorway. Bexley could envision how the woman's narrow features and high cheek bones made her favorable runway material. But it appeared she was recovering from a wild night on the town. *Celebrating a successful heist, perhaps?*

A tawny Chihuahua with a pink bow secured to a collar yipped beside Simone's ankle. "Are you a cop?" she grumbled, side-eying Bexley.

"Is there a reason you would expect one to come knocking on your door?" Bexley quipped.

Simone scooped the dog up from the floor, petting it with a frown. "Who are you?"

"My name's Bexley Squires. I have a few questions about Saturday's fashion show."

"I already talked to that blonde chick that hired me," Simone snapped while continuing to stroke the little dog's head. "What else do you want me to say?"

And Kiersten described this girl as a sweetheart. "I'm a private investigator," Bexley explained. "I may have some questions that Kiersten didn't think of asking." She glanced between the siblings. "Can I come in?"

"Hell yeah!" Travis exclaimed, stepping aside. With a click of her tongue, Simone smacked his arm.

The apartment's living room resembled a high school boy's bedroom. Game controllers and gadgets piled in front of a flatscreen TV, pizza box and food crumbs covered the carpet, crumpled clothes littered the furniture, the smell of something decaying permeated the stale air. Judging by the pillow and sheet covering the couch, Bexley assumed Travis's residency was temporary.

"You're such a pig, Travis!" Simone scolded, kicking a stack of empty energy drinks aside. "And you seriously still wonder why your landlord kicked you out of your house?" She swiped a hooded sweatshirt off a worn leather chair, and threw it across the room before plopping down.

"I'm jonesing for a pizza," Travis announced. He pointed at Bexley. "What flavor you hungry for, Begsley?"

Bexley stood in the center of the room, fearful that the furniture may contain fleas. "I'm good." When Travis sauntered into the kitchen, Bexley turned to Simone. "Did you notice a weight difference in the earrings between rehearsal and the night of the show?"

The girl's bony shoulders rose. "Felt the same to me."

"Do you remember seeing anyone who didn't

belong in that area? Maybe a boyfriend of one of the models, or anyone trying too hard to blend in?"

"I mean there was this photographer who was up in our faces the whole time." Simone tilted her head and squinted. "I wanted to punch the guy. He was *so* annoying."

A snort stuck in Bexley's throat. "Was he *hired* to take pictures of the event?"

"Well…yeah. I guess."

Running her fingertips back and forth along her forehead, Bexley willed herself to remain patient. She guessed the girl was several fries short of a Happy Meal. "What about the security guard you handed them off to? Do you remember anything unusual he may've done or said? Did he seem…on edge? Maybe you noticed him glancing over his shoulder often, or saw his eyes darting around the room more than necessary?"

"Are you suggesting *Nick* stole the earrings?" Simone let out a sharp laugh, causing the dog to pin its ears back. "Oh, that's a good one!"

So they were on a first-name basis. Bexley's eyebrows rose. "You must know this 'Nick' pretty well."

Simone's gaze darted to the corner of the room. "It wasn't the first time we worked together."

"What would make you believe he didn't steal them?"

"Nick's a goodie-two-shoes. He served in the Marine Corps, has a perfect wife and kids, does community service, blah blah blah." Hand waving through the air, she rolled her eyes. "The guy's *literally* a Boy Scout leader for his son. Stealing something worth that much is beyond his skill set. *Trust* me."

The only thing Bexley was willing to trust was that the girl was deliberately trying to downplay her relationship with the security guard.

CHAPTER FIVE

On the way to Nick Harvey's house in Fullerton, Bexley placed several calls. The first was intended to let Brewer know she'd be joining him later than expected, but he didn't answer the burner phone. She dictated a quick text instead.

Then she called Red, requesting a copy of Travis and Simone's criminal histories. It was normally a task within Bexley's purview, but she was spreading herself thin, and time was of the essence with Kiersten's case. Besides, Red was more than happy to comply.

Next up was Temperance Rose.

"*¡Hola, Miss Bexley!*" the reality star trilled. "To what do I owe this pleasure?"

"Temperance, hi. I hate to ask this of you, but my circle of friends with a significant cash flow is limited to you, and only you. But don't worry, what I'm asking doesn't actually involve the *spending* of money. More like a temporary deposit to cover a little white lie for a friend in trouble. I'll return every last cent…with interest."

Without hesitation, Temperance answered, "How much, and where do I send it?"

Her confidence in Bexley felt misplaced—using Temperance's influence with the jeweler was the only temporary solution to Kiersten's conundrum. "Just like that? What if I told you the money was for hookers and blow?"

Her tinkling laugh vibrated against Bexley's ear. "That concept is a little outdated." There was a beat of silence, then, "I'd do anything for you, Miss Bexley. I owe you everything."

"You already paid me for my services, Temperance."

"I don't think you understand. I was a complete *wreck* before you recovered my sweet *Cenicienta's* collar. I worried there was no one left to trust in this world. What you did gave me hope. *La creencia.*"

Bexley thanked Temperance several times and

walked her through the details, then made the most difficult of the three phone calls.

Grayson answered, "You've finally decided to return my calls."

The tightness that stretched through Bexley's chest was impossible to ignore. Though a part of her ached to be reunited with the first man she'd ever truly cared about, it was likely they'd only fall back into the same old routine after a brief honeymoon stage. And masochism wasn't her thing. "This is actually a business call."

"I see," he answered coldly. "Can't give me another chance, but you have no problem still asking for favors."

"This involves Kiersten. She's in trouble, and needs our help."

He released a heavy sigh. "I'm listening."

"Have you ever dealt with counterfeit jewelry?"

"Not personally, but I know a thing or two."

"Where would someone have to go in order to have it created?" she asked.

"That kind of thing is everywhere now. Customs seizes millions of dollars' worth of the stuff every year."

"I'm talking about duplicating a specific piece

of vintage jewelry. Namely, a pair of emerald earrings."

Grayson was quiet for a moment. "I know a guy in the area who served time for counterfeit, and may be able to point us in the right direction. He just happens to owe me a favor. Do you have a picture of the jewelry?"

"I'm on my way to meet with a witness. Give me an hour, and I can provide him with the actual counterfeit earrings."

"My lieutenant is having me look into an under-cover drug bust that went south, so I'll be working late. You can bring the earrings by the station. It'll give us a chance to finally talk."

"I don't have time for that, Grayson." Her SUV's navigation system announced she had arrived at her destination. "I'm sorry, but I really have to go."

She hit "end" on the navigation screen before pulling into the cracked driveway. The neighbor-hood was a significant step down from Simone's, peppered with abandoned houses and junk cars parked on neglected lawns. The Harveys' ranch-style home was on par with the others, in need of new siding and shingles, the front door barely hanging by its hinges. The idea that Nick Harvey had served his country and was now living in such a dismal environment sent waves of empathy rushing through Bexley as she started for the house.

In the backyard, a fit, muscle-bound blonde man tossed a baseball at a little boy with identical features who couldn't have been more than five. The boy held his mitt high in the air with both hands, missing it by more than a yard. The man covered his face and moaned like his kid just blew his shot at the big leagues.

"Nick Harvey?" Bexley called out.

The man's head jerked in Bexley's direction. "Depends who's askin'," he answered with a slight East Coast accent.

"My name's Bexley Squires. I'm a private investigator, hired by SoFetch. Do you have a minute to answer a few questions about the fashion show last weekend?"

He plucked a can of cheap beer from the grass by his feet, eyebrows raised and lips quirked with a grin as he looked Bexley over from head to toe. "Why didn't they call the police?"

"They're hoping to recover the earrings quietly."

"Sure. Guess I got time for you." He motioned

to the kid. "Go inside, Junior. Tell yer ma to start dinner. I'm starving."

The boy dropped his glove where he was standing and raced to the house. Nick took a sip of the beer as he watched his son slip inside. His L.A. Angels t-shirt crept up past a "devil dog" tattoo on his bicep. "That one's not the brightest bulb. Got his smarts from his ma. Surprised that woman was able to graduate high school."

So much for having a perfect wife and kids, Bexley thought as she crossed her arms. "Do you remember anything standing out as unusual that night? Was anyone acting peculiar? Did anything unexpected happen? Did anyone without authorization come backstage?"

"Not that I saw. Felt like your typical rich assholes' night." Returning the can to his lips, he shrugged. "I've been doing this job a long time. This kind of thing hasn't happened on my watch before now."

"How well do you know the other guards hired for the event?"

"Pretty good. Been workin' for the company for almost twenty years."

"Do you think any of them are capable of pulling off a job of this caliber?"

Nick guzzled the last of his beer and pitched the can toward the dilapidated garage before raising a crooked brow. "You sayin' them ugly earrings were worth a lot?"

"Would they have asked you to handle them if they weren't?" Bexley countered.

He shoved a hand into his jeans and gave a one-shouldered shrug. "Most my coworkers are idiots, but they're overall stand-up kind of guys. I don't see any of them getting involved." He started for the garage. "I'm grabbin' another beer. You want one?"

"No thank you." Bexley trailed after him. "What about the model wearing the earrings?"

He spun around, his expression hard. "What *about* her?"

It was exactly the kind of response Bexley had hoped to provoke. There was no doubt in her mind that the two were romantically involved. "Do you think she could've swapped them out when you weren't looking?"

"With what Simone was wearing that night?" Darkness clouded his gaze before he stomped the remaining distance to the garage. He mumbled, "They barely covered her damn tits."

Jealous lover? Checkmate. "I suppose you're right. I spoke with Simone earlier, and she doesn't seem competent to execute this kind of thing. She said the same thing about you."

"Is that so?" Nick sneered, violently yanking the handle of the garage door.

"SoFetch has authorized me to offer a reward for the return of the earrings." It was an outright lie, but one Bexley suspected may propel him into action. She handed him a business card. "If you can think of anything else notable about that night, please give me a call."

THE MOMENT BEXLEY STEPPED INTO KIERSTEN'S high-rise office in downtown L.A., her friend hustled around her desk to wrap Bexley in her arms. "God, I love you!"

Although it still wasn't Bexley's first nature to hug it out, she was becoming accustomed to Kiersten's affection. She lightly squeezed her back. "When did you become polyamorous? Does Luke know?"

Giggling, Kiersten stepped back. "The representative from Shantel de Ellis just called to let me know the earrings don't need to be returned quite yet. Apparently an 'interested buyer' from the area put a hold on the earrings and will be coming by my office this Friday with her assessor to take a look at them. They wanted me to keep them since this buyer insisted my office is a more convenient location."

Bexley shrugged. "Temperance Rose was more than willing to help out. Hopefully it'll give us enough time to find the real pair." She lifted an eyebrow. "I think I may already be onto something. Your model, Simone, lives with a brother who has a pretty extensive criminal history. Not only that, but it seems Simone and the security guard who handled the earrings that night know each other on an intimate level."

Kiersten's eyes rounded. "No way!"

"Way."

"I can't believe you were able to come up with all that information in just a few hours. You should really consider adding 'magician' to your resume."

"And overcome my leporiphobia?" Bexley snorted. "Not a chance."

Kiersten's eyes narrowed. "What do lepers have to do with magic?"

"It means a fear of *rabbits*. Haven't you ever seen *Donny Darko*? Nightmares for days."

"Well, all phobias aside, you really are amazing." She returned to her desk and opened a drawer, sighing. "Grayson called a little bit ago. I wish the two of you would get your shit together, Bex. I'm starting to feel like the child of a bad divorce, having to pass messages between you. Next you'll be fighting over who gets me on the holidays." Frowning, she produced a small velvet box. "Anyway, he told me you'd be stopping by for these."

Without a word, Bexley accepted the box, opening it to survey the contents. To her unexperienced eyes, she'd never know the earrings weren't made with real emeralds. "I'll do everything I can to get the real pair back, Kiersten."

With glistening eyes, Kiersten's lips spread into a deep smile. "I know you will."

By the time Bexley pulled into her apartment's parking lot well after dusk, file folder containing pictures of the deceased men in hand, she was too exhausted to go into the details of Brewer's rendezvous to Mikey's bar. She hadn't spoken to him since early morning. She was starting to wonder if he was still sleeping off the events of the weekend, or if he'd stumbled into more trouble.

As she started for the building, she felt a small flicker of déjà vu. They never did find out who'd made an attempt on her life in the parking lot outside the condo she'd shared with Cineste. Who's to say the shooter wouldn't come for her again? She could still vividly recall the sounds of bullets whizzing past her head. Clenched by a bout of paranoia, she sprinted the remaining distance.

Inside the safety of her dark apartment, she bolted the door behind her and leaned against the wall, willing her heart to slow. *Would she ever conquer the fear of being a target as long as she was in the PI business?* A part of her deeply doubted she'd ever have peace of mind again.

After peering out the window to ensure she wasn't followed, she set the file and her handbag on the kitchen island before flicking the light switch. Several bottles of empty beer were lined up beside the sink, and the door to the guest room down the hallway was still closed.

"Brewer? You here?"

Her question went unanswered for hardly a single heartbeat before there was a knock at the front door. Adrenaline seared through her veins. If

Brewer was in fact a fugitive, a visitor was the last thing they needed. Sighing heavily, she crept over to the peephole. Grayson stood outside her door, a bottle of her favorite Moscato in hand.

To her utter dismay, he looked exceptionally good. Maybe even better than when they'd been together. His thick hair was recently trimmed with an upgrade to the razor-sharp part he'd had when they were first reunited. The longer length perfectly blended with his well-trimmed dark beard. He wore the jeans she loved that just slightly hung off his hips, and perfectly cupped his muscular behind, paired with the weathered Nirvana t-shirt that best showcased his abs and toned biceps. She adored how that shirt looked on him, and how the exceptionally soft material felt against her cheek. Along with the howling wolf inked on his forearm, she was hit with a plethora of memories almost too intense to process.

"Damn you!" she whispered.

Then her breath hitched. *Was Grayson behind the reason Brewer hadn't answered her calls? Did he know she was hiding Brewer from the sheriff?*

"I saw you run inside," Grayson called out. "I'm not leaving until we talk."

Deciding she needed to know if he was onto

them, she glanced over at the bottles. If Grayson didn't already know about Brewer, there could be clues everywhere. She only hoped Brewer would be smart enough to lay low once he heard a man's voice.

She cracked the door open a few inches. "I won't even bother asking how you know where I live." After all, Kiersten made a point of mentioning the conversation she'd had with Grayson, and how she felt about the break-up.

His thick lips playfully quirked, making Bexley's knees weak. "After your call earlier, I figured you'd need something to help you unwind." He thrust the light blue bottle into her arms. "I arranged for you to meet with Craig Roth—ten o'clock tomorrow morning, PS strip mall's south parking lot. The guy's a little skittish, but he's eager to take a look at those earrings."

There was no rational way she could stay mad at the man. He'd even been thoughtful enough to chill the bottle beforehand. Even back in high school, he'd always been so good to her. Better than she deserved. "Thank you."

Grayson slipped his hands into his jeans pockets. "Are you gonna let me in?"

She shook her head. "Sorry, but you're right…

I've had a long day. Besides, I don't know what can be said that we haven't tried to hash out already."

His brown eyes twinkled in the light above her door. "What if I promise to leave as soon as you're done with your first glass?"

"You might want to get your memory tested, Rivers. You forget I out-chugged every guy on the football team at our graduation party." It had been out of character for Bexley at the time, but she was simply glad to be done with Papaya Springs for good. *Or so she thought.* She pushed the door and stepped aside. "Go crazy, I guess."

It physically pained her to witness as he quickly scrutinized the place. She crossed her arms over her clenched stomach, suspecting he resented every square inch of her cramped apartment. Since she hadn't taken the time to decorate in the several months since she'd moved in, she worried he'd take that as a sign that she wasn't intending to stay. A sign that gave him false hope.

"Hope your rent's not too steep," he said. "It's...small."

Sighing heavily, she closed the door behind him. "It's close to the office. Besides, I'm hardly ever home these days." Turning away, she started for the cupboard. "Do you want a glass?"

His eyes darted to the empty bottles. "You're drinking IPA now?" he asked, his voice laced with skepticism.

"It was all I had on hand. I'd bought it in case Alex stopped over." Truthfully, she'd purchased a six-pack several weeks back, intending to invite Alex and her sister for dinner. But when she imagined Cineste's reaction to the fact that she was no longer with Grayson, she'd changed her mind. No use shattering her sister's belief that happily ever after was a tangible concept.

"I'll take an IPA, if you have any left." Grayson plopped down onto an island stool. "Those two still hot and heavy?"

"They're not officially engaged, but they're already making plans for a wedding." Inside the fridge, one bottle remained. She popped the top, then handed it to Grayson.

His fingers trapped hers against the bottle. "You don't know how badly I wish that was us." His dark eyes twinkled with emotion. "Suppose you'll ever forgive me for being an overbearing jerk?"

"It's not just that, Gray." She slipped her fingers from his grip. "You want the whole family package—a stay-at-home wife…kids. I'm not sure any of that's for me. You're a good man. You deserve to be with someone who wants the same things."

"I get it. If you decide that's not what you want, I guess I could somehow learn to adjust if that's the only way this can work." He leaned back, jaw held tight. "These last few weeks have been pure torture."

"These last few weeks *happened* because I can't have you micromanaging my life." Her tongue felt dry and heavy when she attempted to wet her lips. "I can't deal with your temper every time I take on another dangerous case."

"I won't lie. It made me livid, but only because I couldn't wrap my head around the idea of losing you. I've since come to terms with the fact that I can't stand in your way of anything." His gaze slid down to the beer bottle. "I can't even look at another woman without wondering whether or not you've moved on with someone else. Maybe we should try couples therapy. I'm willing to do whatever it takes, because I sure as hell can't stand the idea of a life without you." Looking back at her, his voice cracked when he added, "I love you, Bex."

Throat thick with emotion, she glanced down at her feet. She still cared immensely about Grayson and probably always would. She knew that much to be true. Regardless of her feelings, she was horrified that Brewer could be listening in on every word of their conversation.

"I can't…I don't know how to—"

"I think I better go." With a steely expression, Grayson pushed the untouched beer away, and stood. He held Bexley's gaze for a moment, lips parting with one last thought. But he snapped them back shut, and trudged away.

Bexley turned her head, hoping he hadn't noticed the tears forming in her eyes.

"I'm just gonna use your bathroom," he called out, "then I'll be on my way."

Her pulse throbbed against her neck as she looked up. "Not that one!"

It was too late. He had already opened the door to the guest bedroom.

But Brewer was gone.

CHAPTER SIX

For the second night in a row, Bexley hardly slept more than a handful of hours. Once she'd searched every sparse inch of her apartment after Grayson left, she'd called Mikey's bar to confirm what she'd already feared: Brewer's bike was no longer parked outside. She laid awake for hours, contemplating whether she should search for him, or trust that he knew what he was doing.

Shortly before sunlight breached her bedroom window, she made the decision that regardless of Brewer's location, he was still her client. Unless he instructed her otherwise, she would continue her investigation.

Once settled in at Stronghold Investigations, her first task was to call PS Security to confirm Nick

Harvey had been with their company for over nineteen years. The woman Bexley spoke to in PR stated that Nick was considered a stellar employee. Although unwilling to disclose any specific information from his file, the woman told her their hiring policy ensured employees didn't possess a record involving a gross misdemeanor or felony.

A quarter after nine, Red literally skipped into Bexley's office, bright red hair pinned on either side of her head in Princess-Leia-style buns, laptop clasped under one arm, neon green T-shirt featuring a cartoon character—Bexley thought maybe it was one of those Italian brothers from that old school video game.

"Mornin', boss-lady!"

"Good morning, zany contracted employee," Bexley quipped in return.

Red marched around to Bexley's side once again, and set a small pile of paper on the desk. "Here are those records you requested. Simone's includes a minor consumption at eighteen, and a misdemeanor possession of coke a few months back. Travis has a long rap sheet that involves small-time dealing throughout the past decade, and a couple gross misdemeanor thefts that were reduced to misdemeanors. Guy sounds one rock short of being an Ewok. He got caught both times during daylight hours, stealing out in the wide open."

"Hardly the history of an elaborate miscreant," Bexley agreed, even though she had no idea what Red meant by Ewok. "I'd like you to dig around later, see what kind of personal information you can find on these two, as well as on a man by the name of Nicholas Harvey who works for PS Security. But first, I need to see the Currie County roster." Wondering whether or not Sheriff Blair had gotten his hands on Brewer was one of the worries that had kept Bexley awake in the night.

Red's fingers, nails still painted the sparkling silver, flew across the keyboard as Bexley spoke. "Roster's on its way to the printer," she reported with a proud smile.

"You're insanely efficient. And possibly a little insane for not taking the FBI job." Bexley exhaled deeply, feeling weighted by guilt. "I can't begin to afford to pay you what your services are actually worth."

Still typing, Red lifted a shoulder. "I've been told I'm clinically insane for a number of reasons that have nothing to do with my refusal to become one of the FBI's drones."

File that one under "things better left unsaid", Bexley decided. "Before you look into the others, I'd like you to see what you can dig up on a Brewer Hawkins, born in this county back in November of ninety, enlisted in the Coast Guard around oh-eight. I want his medical, financial, military, and criminal histories."

Since Brewer had left without any explanation, she planned to fill herself in on every last detail of his life. With any luck, she'd be able to fill in the blank spaces, starting with why he lived in a motel named after a shameless douche. Though she hated prying into his business without his knowledge, he'd left her no other choice.

Bexley snagged her handbag from the back of her chair, and looped it across her body. "I'm headed out for an appointment with an expert on counterfeit jewelry. If you could send a quick rundown on a convicted felon from Papaya Springs named Craig Roth to my phone in the next ten minutes, I'd be especially grateful. I just need a superficial history to verify I'm not going to meet with Ted Bundy's protégé."

Not that Bexley thought Grayson would set her up to meet with a violent criminal. It merely seemed like common sense. Then again, after the way Grayson stormed out of her apartment the night before, she wasn't so sure he wouldn't take some pleasure in seeing her tortured. Even if just for a little while.

Red's eyes didn't stray from her laptop's screen. "I got you, sister. No way I'm lettin' you wander into a sith's lair."

Rather than asking Red to explain, Bexley merely shook her head on her way out. She supposed the mind of a gifted genius wasn't always an easy map to follow.

WHILE WAITING FOR CRAIG ROTH TO APPEAR AT the location arranged by Grayson, Bexley was able to breathe a little easier. The jail roster hadn't included Brewer, and Red's search revealed Mr. Roth's convictions were entirely of a non-violent nature—counterfeit of merchandise, theft, racketeering, etc.

Then she spotted Grayson's classic white Bronco pulling into the strip mall parking lot. A rusted out Chevy Nova with its bumper duct taped in place trailed closely behind. Her stomach churned with the breakfast burrito she'd grabbed after leaving the office. *Of course he'd insist on being present.*

After Grayson and the other car parked two rows away, the two men ambled toward Bexley, deep in conversation. Grayson wore a wrinkled black shirt with cargo shorts and flip flops. His thick hair was ruffled, and darkness marred his uncharacteristically dull brown eyes. It looked as if he hadn't slept.

His companion, a middle aged man, wore his dark hair in thin wisps against his liver spotted scalp. His eyes were also rimmed with darkness, only his seemed to be the product of a haunted past. His build was similar to that of a mall variety Santa Claus, though it was unlikely he'd ever land such a gig based on the frightening tattoos that covered his neck. He shuffled his feet as if they were chained together—possibly a habit he'd developed in the ten plus years he'd spent incarcerated.

Bexley slipped outside to meet them, leaning against her SUV with her arms crossed. Before she could say anything to Grayson, he met her scowl, hands held up.

"I'm here as a civilian. I'm equally invested in helping Kiersten."

Fair enough. Bexley eyed the other man. "You must be Craig."

The man shifted his stance, emitting the stench of B.O. and cigarettes. "That's right," he answered in a high, pinched voice.

She dug into her handbag, producing the velvet box. "What can you tell me about these earrings?"

Craig took the box and opened it with trembling hands. Eyes narrowed, he held it closer to his face. "These were made by somebody with a whole lotta experience." He removed one to inspect the backside. "They used copper combined with other metals. The stones are synthetic, created by either hydrothermal or Flux-fusion lab process. But the soldering process was done in a hurry—they got sloppy."

Bexley glanced Grayson's way. "Kiersten said they'd only known for a few weeks that these earrings would be used in the fashion show. The thief would've requested a rush order." She turned back to Craig. "Any idea who might've made them?"

"I know a couple'a guys around here." He wiped a hand across his forehead. "They sure ain't gonna wanna talk to any investigators."

"Then you can talk to them yourself," Grayson

told him. "See if they're willing to give you a description of the customer that ordered them. We're not after the jeweler unless he's the one who physically stole the originals."

Bexley produced a business card from her handbag. "Give me a call if you get any leads, Mr. Roth. And spread the word to any contacts of yours involved in fencing jewelry—there's a hefty reward out for the return of the originals."

Craig snatched the card from her fingers, his eyes shifting between Grayson and Bexley. "If anyone asks where you got this information, we never met." He scurried back to his midnight blue car like a cockroach exposed to light.

"You didn't have to come along." Bexley told Grayson, her tone somewhere between appreciation and scolding.

"This isn't about you needing protection," he clarified. "I took the day off, hoping to take some of the pressure off you in whatever way you need. I want to do everything in my power to save Kiersten's job."

That was certainly unexpected. Bexley wet her lips as she processed the idea. "Your lieutenant gave you the day off?"

"Baker's been goading me to take time off ever

since his daughter was in the hospital." His eyes drifted across the parking lot. "He's always preaching how no one should take family for granted."

Curse words burned against Bexley's lips. He was playing dirty, and he knew it. "See what you can do to get the security footage from the event center. They gave Kiersten some lame excuse when she requested it." She squared her shoulders back. Bossing Grayson around for a change, rather than vice versa, was exhilarating. "Stop by my office once it's in your possession, and we'll review it together. I'll give you a rundown of a theory I'm working on that involves the model who wore the earrings and a security guard."

He dipped his chin. "Assuming I can have it by lunchtime, I'll bring tacos."

Arms sternly crossed, she narrowed her eyes. Grayson was fully aware that tacos were her biggest weakness. "It's gonna take more than tacos to change my mind about us, Rivers."

"Even if they're from Pollo's?" he asked, raising a lone eyebrow.

In the span of time they'd dated, Grayson had taken her to her mom's favorite restaurant on so many occasions that the elderly Mexican immigrant owner had become a valued friend. Bexley set her hands on her hips, scowling as he started walking backwards toward his car with a mischievous grin. She secretly loved that he was the only one who knew Pollo's tacos were her biggest weakness.

"I won't forget the extra queso!" he called out with a wink.

RED CAME RUSHING OUT FROM BEHIND BEXLEY'S desk at Stronghold Investigations the moment she saw her new boss. "O.M.G. This Brewer Hawkins man is hella hot *and* loaded. Had I stumbled over him under any other circumstances, I'd be slipping him my number and doodling his name on my notebook."

While it wasn't exactly new information, Bexley was curious as to Red's definition of "loaded." She set her handbag on the corner of the desk to take the stack of papers Red offered.

"Mr. Hawkins possesses both a perfect bill of health, and a mild criminal record," Red explained. "There was an assault that was dismissed, and a few warnings for traffic violations. He served four years with the Coast Guard right out of high school, and worked various jobs for a couple of years before starting an auto repair business. You ready for the most interesting part?" Red's lips twisted with a grin. "Aside from his income from those two legit sources, Mr. Dreamy once had several offshore accounts that he'd been hiding from Uncle Sam. The numbers between his business and the accounts don't match up. At one point, he was worth *millions*. The dude made serious bank elsewhere."

Bexley's throat worked against a gasp. There wasn't any possible way her humble friend was worth that amount. *Red must've made a mistake.* Trying to maintain a straight face, she thumbed through the printouts, coming across dozens of hospital bills for an ISABELLA ROMANO. She held one up for Red to see. "Who's this?"

"No idea, but this Brewer dreamboat paid hundreds of thousands of dollars for her care at Papaya Springs General. The bills stopped two years ago once the account zeroed out. Shortly after, he anonymously donated a large amount into an account for kids in Currie County foster care." Red let out a dramatic sigh. "A man with a heart like that?" She covered her hands over her heart.

"Take my ovaries already, Mr. Hawkins. They're yours!"

As badly as Bexley wanted to scold the girl on professionalism in the work place, she had to admit Red had a point. She'd never met a single millionaire who didn't own expensive toys or an impressive mansion. Beyond Brewer's motorcycle, which he used as his sole form of transportation, he seemingly had nothing.

Who was Isabella Romano, and why did Brewer have a soft spot for children in the system?

Red handed Bexley more printouts. "I also gathered the deets you wanted on the other three. There's not a lot to report about Nicholas Harvey. He served as a Marine sniper shortly after his twenty-first birthday, including a tour in Afghanistan. Then he got married, created a little family, and took the job with PS Security. His credit is horrible, thanks to some past gambling debt and frequent visits to a local strip club. Probably explains why he attends couples therapy with the missus twice a week. Criminal history is limited to a pair of misdemeanor assaults that resulted in a thirty day jail sentence, and a DUI charge a few months before he enlisted that was eventually dismissed. My guess? The judge on the case was a veteran who gave him an ultimatum."

Based on the information, Bexley decided it was logical that Nick would be interested in a young, attractive model who didn't require money to entertain.

When Red produced a thicker mound of papers, her eyes sparked to life. "The Paxton siblings, on the other hand, are an interesting duo. Simone flunked out of high school, and waitressed at three upscale restaurants between Go-Sees and acting auditions. She was finally signed on a few years back by a modeling agency, but her actual gigs have been sparse. She doesn't earn nearly enough to afford her current rent. It would seem *Travis* inherited all the family wisdom because he graduated second in his class with a four-point-twelve, and scored fifteen-fifty on the SAT. We're talking close to genius level."

"No way," Bexley said, snatching the papers from Red's hand. "The Travis Paxton I know couldn't tie his own shoelaces." It suddenly dawned on her—with an IQ that high, what if Travis *wanted* people to believe he was a mindless stoner? "Thanks for this information, Red. You can take off for now. I'll holler if I need you for anything else."

As much as the girl had helped in the past twenty-four hours, Bexley wished J.J. had the resources to hire her full time.

"If I don't hear from you by the end of the week, I'll send my bill," Red told her with a nod. Then a loud ding sounded from her laptop. She plopped down in Bexley's chair and flipped the screen up, frowning. "Hold on. I set an alert under Mr. Dreamy's name. Something just triggered it."

Bexley's pulse quickened as Red's fingers did their thing. As hard as she'd tried not to dwell on Brewer's location all morning, his wellbeing was always nagging the forefront of her mind. "What is it?"

"Oh boy." Red sat back in Bexley's chair, lacing her fingers over her head. "Guess this would explain why he's loaded."

Bexley tried to position herself behind Red, so she could read the screen, but it remained black. "Damn it, Red. I'm chucking your super-secret spy computer across the room if you don't tell me what's up!"

"Currie County just issued a warrant for Brewer's arrest." Eyebrows arched, Red turned to face her. "The sheriff found several bricks of cocaine in a storage shed registered in his name."

CHAPTER SEVEN

Nausea blazed through Bexley's chest as she paced across her office. Red left a printout of the warrant so Bexley could review the evidence for herself. Based on an anonymous tip, Sheriff Blair and his goons had raided the storage facility located four blocks from Dick's Inn earlier that morning. The property manager confirmed the unit had been rented in Brewer's name two years prior, and he'd even spotted Brewer leaving the parking lot as the sun was rising several hours before he was interviewed.

It only validated Bexley's worst fears: (1) she wasn't as skilled at the private detective gig as everyone believed, and (2) she couldn't trust anyone…no matter how much she believed in them. When she'd confronted Brewer about his situation the night they returned from Mexico, he implied that he had done some "crooked shit" that he regretted. Was that his subliminal way of admitting he was into drug trafficking?

Her less cynical side wondered the legitimacy of the situation. She had once been falsely accused of murdering a woman, and Sheriff Blair had been determined to crucify Bexley without solid evidence. Maybe like her story, Brewer had stuck his nose where it didn't belong, and angered someone powerful.

She wanted to believe there was more to his story.

Desperate for answers, she fired off a set of texts to the burner phone.

> *Where are you?*
> *We need to talk ASAP!*
> *Please.*

The borrowed time she'd managed to allot Kiersten was running out. She needed to focus on Travis's backstory, and spend less time wondering if she'd been betrayed by a friend. It was bad enough she had believed Dean Halliwell's portrayal of innocence when he was in fact a psychopathic serial killer. Grayson and J.J. would lose all faith in her if they discovered she'd been chumming around with a suspected drug lord.

The office phone buzzed with an intercom message, startling Bexley.

"Your handsome gentleman caller is here, Miss Squires. I'm sending him back."

Bexley was neither in the mood for correcting the sweet old woman especially as she had been sick for over a week, nor was she up for entertaining Grayson as if nothing was amiss. But she needed to see whatever Grayson had found.

With the start of a headache banging against her temples, she lifted the handset to say, "Thanks, Leona. Hope you're feeling better today."

"I don't know…I just can't seem to shake this cold."

As she hung up, Grayson nudged the door open. With the sight of his handsome, unassuming smile, Bexley nearly crumpled to the floor. For the first time since they'd parted ways, she yearned for his comfort, and wished he'd wrap her in his arms…tell her everything would be okay. Even though she was strong enough to take care of herself, she had to admit there were a lot of situations she wouldn't have survived if it weren't for her network of friends. If it weren't for *Grayson* in particular.

His brow wrinkled as he closed the door. "What's wrong?"

Glancing at the two white Pollo's bags clasped in his fist, her stomach growled. In light of Brewer's news, she'd forgotten Grayson's promise to deliver her favorite. "It seems I'm what the kids now days call 'hangry'." She met his gaze. "Did you get the footage?"

He set the bags on her desk and nodded. "At first the manager tried to give me the runaround. Once I flashed my badge, he was quick to accommodate my request."

Bexley ran her bottom lip between her teeth, releasing it with a quiet *pop*. "I'm working on a new theory, but I don't want to say anything until we've watched the feed. I want your feedback first."

"Sit down and eat," he commanded. "I'll get it going on your laptop."

She dug into the first bag, grinning with the

sight of Pollo's familiar handwriting scrawled in black grease pen on the first taco she grabbed.

For mi amiga Bexley with extra queso. Have a nice day. :)

She wasn't surprised to find her favorite pineapple flavored Mexican soda in the second bag alongside Grayson's favorite lemon-lime. She set the remaining two tacos on the other side of the desk, and began indulging in her delicious taco while Grayson stuck a USB stick into the side of her MacBook. With a few quick clicks, Grayson had the security footage up and rolling.

Four different angles appeared on a split screen. Two appeared to show opposite sides of the stage where chairs were arranged for the audience, and two more recorded different areas backstage. At the time of the recording, the facility was empty aside from a handful of clothing racks.

"Kiersten didn't have access to the venue until eight o'clock that morning," Grayson explained as he sat across from Bexley, "so that's when they started the recording."

"This will take *hours* to review," Bexley grumbled.

With a taco in hand, Grayson bent forward to

type something into the computer. The digital clock displayed at the top of the videos sped up until minutes became seconds. "Holler if you see anything, and I can slow it down or go back."

While chewing the last of her taco, Bexley rubbed at her aching temple and checked her phone to see if Brewer had replied. She didn't know how long she could be locked inside her office with Grayson before she lost her mind. It wasn't her style to sit around when there were cases that needed solving.

"You need to look into a desktop monitor, Bex. Staring all day at this little screen is going to give you migraines. I can have the IT guy at the station hook you up."

"I can manage," she said before slugging down her soda. She kind of dug the fact that he was still looking out for her welfare, but she could have Red set her up with better equipment.

She opened the file she'd created for Kiersten's case and angled it for Grayson to see. "These are the three main players we want to keep an eye out for." She pointed at the picture of Nick in uniform that Red pulled off PS Security's website. "This is the security guard assigned to the earrings." She thumbed through the papers until she found a headshot of Simone. "This is the model who wore them." Then she found one of Travis's mugshots. "And this is the model's brother. His involvement in this heist is under question." Her eyes flickered back to her laptop as Kiersten appeared on the footage. "We can't rule anyone out at this point, but my money's on these suspects. It's possible they were even working together."

Grayson nodded. "Noted. How's Kiersten holding up?"

"She sent a text earlier to see if I had any new information, and commented that she was feeling optimistic about my involvement. I have a feeling she only said it as a way to assure herself I have more skills than a talking dog and his stoner friend."

Grayson reached across her desk, curling one of his large hands around hers. "Don't you dare start doubting yourself again," he scolded with a hard look. "We've been through this too many times. Solving cases is your calling, Bex. No one who does it for a living is perfect."

Warmth from his touch zinged up her arm, settling in her spine. It was the spark of assurance she'd been wanting since he stepped inside her office. It was also a glimpse of what she could have if she'd stop being too stubborn to give him another chance. Her mouth became dry as she held his stare, wondering if she was crazy for resisting the love and affection of a kind, hardworking man.

She intended to ask him if he wanted to come by her place later when her cell phone dinged several times, interrupting their moment. She withdrew her hand from Grayson's to find a string of texts from the burner phone she'd given Brewer.

> *Moonlight Falls park @ 5 tonight*
>> *Behind the maintenance shed on south end*
>> *Make sure u r not followed*

Finally, Bexley thought, feeling a rush of relief. At least he was alive.

Then there was a knock on Bexley's office door. By the firm, swift sound, Bexley knew to expect J.J. to come breezing through the doorway. What she wasn't expecting was the stern look her boss threw her before realizing she wasn't alone. He dipped his chin in Grayson's direction as Grayson paused the video.

"Good to see you again, son," J.J. drawled. "What brings you by?"

"He's helping me on a case," Bexley blurted. She wasn't comfortable telling him that she'd neglected all her other cases to assist not only one, but *two* friends in need. Besides, she suspected by the gleam in J.J.'s eyes that he hoped the detective was there on personal business. "What can I help you with, J.J.?"

"Got the Currie County Sheriff's office on the line." Tugging at the diamond stud in his ear, the old man tilted his head. "They're callin' to inquire about your involvement with Brewer Hawkins. Somethin' about you payin' a visit to his room at Big Dick's Inn?"

Bexley's stomach clenched. *Shit. So much for Big Dick's discretion.*

Heat rushed through her cheeks when she felt the weight of Grayson's stare. "You and Hawkins?" he asked, his voice heavy with sarcasm.

Refusing to entertain the question, her eyes remained steady on J.J.. "I have nothing to hide," she insisted, despite the glaring lie. "We're *friends*."

She was relieved Grayson couldn't witness the look of doubt taking over J.J.'s expression. The way his eyebrows raised, she was certain he already made the connection between Brewer and her "friend's" involvement when she had asked about researching a death in Mexico. "Then I'm guessin' you already know about the warrant out for this *friend's* arrest? They're requestin' you pay a visit to their office to answer a few questions."

Expecting Grayson to lay into her about the company she kept in his absence, she was shocked to hear him say, "Considering your track record with Sheriff Blair, it sounds to me like you better pay Luke a visit first." He drummed his fingers against the desk before he stood. "I'll drive."

ALTHOUGH BEXLEY WAS CONVINCED GRAYSON HAD volunteered to come along because he wanted to hear the details of her "relationship" with Brewer, she was grateful for the suggestion. She was even more thankful when Grayson let her know he'd wait in the lobby.

By the time she sat across from Luke in the Jacobs & Johnson Law Firm downtown, he had already placed several crucial calls and received an email from the sheriff's office.

"I can't make sense of this," he told Bexley, running a hand through his thick, jet black hair while studying a piece of paper. "I dug around a little, and cashed in on a few favors to get more information. According to this, the request for the search warrant on Brewer Hawkins's motel room was *verbally* made by the acting district attorney. In the application submitted to the judge, it states the request was made by the sheriff after an anonymous tip was called in."

Bexley held a hand to her mouth, feigning surprise. "You're telling me the powers that be in Papaya Springs may be hiding something? The *horror*."

Luke looked up at her, his friendly brown eyes shining with amusement. "I guess that's not exactly a new flash. But why hide the origin of the request?"

"Hmmm. Considering the stellar elected officials the city attorney represents, it also wouldn't be a revelation to learn there were ulterior motives involved."

"Would you be referring to Mayor Hoffman?" Luke asked, quirking a lone eyebrow.

"What if he decided to come after me again? What if he knows I've been spending time with Brewer? You can't sit there and tell me that would be out of character, all things considered."

"I can agree with you that the mayor might be holding a grudge against you considering your history, but you're beginning to sound a little paranoid." With a sigh, Luke steepled his fingers together. "Bex, if there's anything else I should know about your involvement in Brewer Hawkins's case, *now's* the time to disclose everything." Leaning back in his chair, his eyes flashed in the direction of the hallway. "As my client, this conversation will remain confidential."

Bexley was well aware that in addition to dating her best friend, Luke had a long-running friendship with Grayson. She was also confident that Luke was a professional, and wouldn't indulge in gossip.

"Brewer's become a good friend, but more importantly, he's *my* client," she admitted. "I was hired to investigate something…*unrelated* to the drugs they found in his storage unit." She paused, scraping her bottom lip between her teeth. "Well, at least I first assumed it was unrelated. I was convinced the Brewer Hawkins I'd been spending time with wasn't capable of any wrongdoing. Now…I'm not so sure. Either way, I can't tell the sheriff everything I know about Brewer's situation. At least not until I've looked into a few things."

"How deep are you into this thing?"

"Maybe not as deep as Wille Nelson's love for weed, but close."

Tapping his fingers against his chair, Luke

briefly pressed his lips together, deep in thought. "Do you know his current whereabouts?"

"As of this morning, no."

"Before that?"

She flashed a stiff smile. "Is pleading the fifth to your own lawyer a thing?"

With an unsatisfied grunt, Luke pressed a button on his office phone. "Sharon, call Sheriff Blair's office to let him know I'm bringing Bexley Squires in for questioning, then reschedule my next two appointments."

"I'm on it," Sharon's bright voice answered through the speaker system.

While adjusting his sky blue designer tie, Luke slowly rose to his feet. "We both know that son of a bitch will try his best to prod you into saying something to incriminate yourself. Do me a favor, and don't say anything unless I scribble a reply on my notepad."

"I'll do my best," she answered truthfully, trailing behind him to the doorway. "Although keeping my lips zipped when it comes to defending myself isn't exactly my forte."

Hand on the doorknob, Luke turned to face her. "I mean it. Don't provoke him into holding you any longer than necessary." His brows lowered. "Kiersten is counting on you to save her from the mess she's in."

"You're sweet to worry about her, but I'm getting close," Bexley promised. She wrapped a hand around his arm and gave a gentle squeeze. "Focus on getting the sheriff off my back, and I'll focus on getting my hands on those earrings."

CHAPTER EIGHT

In the sheriff's lair, Grayson and Luke both stood behind Bexley as she checked in with the front desk. She had to admit she drew courage from the fact that the two men supported her no matter what, although her conscience grew heavier every time she caught one of Grayson's terse smiles.

Deputy Danks breezed past, stopping in his tracks when he noticed them. The young deputy greeted Luke and Grayson before he turned to Bexley, his youthful features lifting with a wide smile. "Long time no see, Squires. What brings you here this time?"

"Pictures with the sheriff. I figure I've been spending enough quality time with him that we may as well send out Christmas cards together. You know, to save on postage."

With the sound of several men's deep laughter, Bexley looked over her shoulder as Mayor Hoffman exited the sheriff's office, surrounded by his cronies. The mayor's dark eyes locked with Bexley's, and his jolly expression morphed into a triumphant sneer.

"Anyone else feel a rush of pure adoration?" she asked.

"Don't let him get under your skin," Luke warned.

"Too late," she answered through gritted teeth. "He's already festering in it…like a leper."

Mayor Hoffman continued to hold Bexley's stare for a moment longer before he strolled out with his small entourage in tow. In that moment, Bexley was certain that some way, somehow, the mayor was behind the reason she'd been called in for questioning.

Next to exit the room was Grayson's supervisor. Lieutenant Baker's expression became perplexed when he spotted Grayson. Bexley hadn't seen him since his daughter almost died of alcohol poisoning, courtesy of the sisters at Kappa Kappa Delta. He'd put on a considerable amount of weight since their last encounter, appearing grossly obese, and his dark beard had almost completely turned stark white.

"I thought you were taking the day off, Rivers," Lieutenant Baker scoffed.

Grayson shrugged. "I'm here on a personal matter."

"I gathered as much." The lieutenant's gaze honed in on Bexley. "I was told you've been keeping questionable company."

"What's questionable is the way you're assuming Brewer Hawkins' culpability," Bexley retorted, dipping her chin. "What happened to innocent until proven guilty?"

The lieutenant grunted before turning back to Grayson. "I'll see you in the morning."

He promptly left. Sheriff Blair became the lone man remaining from the conference. The portly man leaned against the door frame of his office, watching Bexley while scratching his chin. She half expected him to twirl the edges of his dark mustache like the villain in a silent film.

"He's all bark and rarely bites," Deputy Danks whispered, patting Bexley's shoulder and chuckling as he walked away.

"Here's hoping he's up to date on his shots," Bexley muttered.

IN THE SAME INTERROGATION ROOM IN WHICH Bexley had been questioned after being kidnapped, drugged, and accused of performing egregious harm to a falsified victim, Sheriff Blair stood rigid behind the metal table. He nudged the edge of his cowboy hat upward, revealing his neatly trimmed hairline. "I'm assuming you brought counsel because you have something to hide."

Bexley held her hand to the side of her mouth. "You know what they say about assumptions, Sheriff. They make an ass outta you and—well, in your case—you."

With a harsh cough, Luke elbowed Bexley's side. He then scribbled on his notepad and held it up for her to read.

zip it! seriously!

"It's my understanding you've become…*close*… with Brewer Hawkins," the sheriff drawled, crossing his arms. "Would this happen to be on an *intimate* level?"

"My client's relationship with Mr. Hawkins is of a professional nature," Luke answered in a sharp tone. "Accordingly, she won't be commenting on their privileged communications."

Sheriff Blair didn't acknowledge him in any way as he continued leering at Bexley. "I've been told you're spending a curious amount of time with Mr. Hawkins. In fact, you were witnessed entering his motel room on *several* occasions. Are you going to sit there and pretend you don't have any knowledge of his criminal activities?"

Bexley propped an elbow on the table and twirled a lock of her brown hair. "Sounds as if you've been keeping close tabs on me, Sheriff. Either you're jonesing to catch me doing something unsavory—and I'm assuming it's on behalf of someone with sinister motives—or you're building up the courage to ask me out." She batted her eyelashes. "If it's the latter, that would explain why you're still single. Stalking is never the right way to win a girl's heart."

Luke pinched the backside of Bexley's bicep, causing her to squeak.

The sheriff's face turned dark red as he held Bexley's stare, stabbing his pointer finger against the table. "What were you doing inside his motel room on Sunday evening?" he demanded. "Are you simply hiding the fact that you're sleeping with a criminal, or are you also involved in trafficking those drugs?"

Luke pushed away from the table and stood. "This isn't an interrogation, it's straight-up harassment. Unless you're going to charge my client with something substantial, we'll be on our way."

Bexley stood along with Luke, throwing the sheriff a terse look before they headed for the exit. She was sure he'd validated her fear that the mayor had been watching her every move. But how much did they know? Would they charge her with harboring a fugitive?

"I'm onto you, Squires!" the sheriff yelled behind them.

From the sharp look Grayson shot her in the hallway, she almost wondered if he'd heard their entire conversation. "Everything good?" he asked through a clenched jaw.

"He doesn't have anything on her," Luke answered. As the trio started back toward the parking lot, he side-eyed Bexley. "Try to lay low. You don't want to give anything that'll make the sheriff more suspicious. And let me know if I can do anything that would expedite Kiersten's case."

"Thanks, Luke," she said before they parted ways.

Grayson was quiet until they climbed into his Bronco. Staring straight ahead, he remained motionless. "Hawkins was at your place last night, wasn't he? That's who'd been drinking the beer. That's why you were so uptight."

Her heart squeezed painfully hard with his betrayed tone. "I didn't tell you because I didn't want to put you in a compromising situation."

When he turned to her, his eyes shone with anger. "But it was okay to humiliate me by letting him hear everything I had to say to you?"

"You basically forced your way in," she reminded him. "Besides, he was long gone by then."

"If you've moved on..." He turned away, palming the back of his neck as his head dropped backward. "I hope you'd have the decency to tell me."

Her stomach dropped as she wet her lips. "I don't know what to tell you, Gray." While nothing physical had transpired between them, Bexley would be lying if she claimed her relationship with Brewer wasn't of any importance. She certainly wasn't in the right state of mind to declare she had feelings for either man. "I just need...some time... and space."

Lips pressed into a tight line, Grayson started the vehicle. They each remained silent for the entire ride back to Stronghold Investigations. In the parking lot, Bexley checked her phone for the time. The park where she was to meet Brewer was on the other side of Papaya Springs, and the trip could take longer than usual with rush hour traffic. She hated leaving Grayson, especially given their last conversation.

"Thanks for the lift," she told him, reaching for the passenger's side handle before he'd killed the engine. "I have to meet with a witness on another case. I'm not sure how long it'll take. We can finish watching the event footage in the morning."

Grayson turned the key and shook his head. "I know how the idle stuff gets on your nerves. I'll head inside and finish it up myself. I'll be just fine without you."

Though she knew what he meant, the words still hit home. As she started for her SUV, a single question burned in the back of her mind. Would *she* be fine without *him*?

BEXLEY MADE IT TO THE MEETING PLACE WITH FIVE minutes to spare. Worried the sheriff had put a tail on her, she'd made unnecessary turns several times.

It was an unusually warm day for the end of October in Papaya Springs, but the park's proximity to the ocean kept it ten degrees cooler than it'd been in the heart of the city. Bexley removed her sandals and sunk her toes into the warm sand before plopping down on a small mound and rolling her slacks up to her knees.

A dozen yards away, a young family worked on building a sandcastle with plastic shovels and buckets. Several small sailboats bounced lazily far off in the distance, and a few young women in wetsuits with skimboards under their arms watched with long faces as weak waves drizzled against the shoreline.

Moonlight Falls Park had been one of Bexley's favorite areas in Papaya Springs for as long as she could remember. The wealthy locals didn't frequent the area because of the seaweed and dead fish that washed to shore throughout the day. The middle class eventually stopped coming because of the stench. The park was known for being quiet, which attributed to its higher participation in the city's crime rate.

Bexley closed her eyes, letting the sun warm her face. The early evening tide had washed away any unsavory odors, filling her lungs with the crisp scent of the ocean. She'd been "burning the candle at both ends" as J.J. called it ever since she returned to Papaya Springs, and was in dire need of a getaway. Preferably to a remote location without WiFi, cell service, or people.

Maybe Kiersten or Cineste would be up for a girls' trip once she'd recovered the earrings and untangled Brewer's mess. She wrapped her arms around her knees, losing herself in the idea of kicking back on a beach in Hawaii with a tropical drink in one hand and an engaging romance novel in the other. Maybe if she broke away from her life for a week or two, she could focus on her feelings for Grayson. She needed to decide once and for all what she wanted out of life, and if he could exist in that vision. Either way, it wasn't fair to leave him in limbo.

The heady scent of tobacco, leather, and masculine soap encompassed her a second before Brewer sank into the sand at her side. He wore black cargo shorts and a gray T-shirt, a ratty baseball cap pulled down to a pair of black Wayfarer sunglasses, motorcycle jacket tucked under one arm. His back was stiff, and his expression was hard. Something was wrong.

Fists clenched in her lap, Bexley stared at the crown tattooed on the back of his hand as he cupped it over a cigarette and lighter. She couldn't decide if she wanted to pull him in close, or knock him out.

"Where have you been?" she snapped.

Once his cigarette was lit, he took a long drag and blew smoke out his nose before turning to her. "Had some stuff to take care of."

"You could've left a note."

"It sounded like you and your boyfriend needed space," he answered, shrugging. "Besides, I wasn't going to let you take the fall for harboring a wanted felon."

Her teeth clamped together. "You know about the warrant."

"I figured somethin' like that would be comin'." He turned to stare out at the ocean, eyes unfocused. "One of my Coastie buddies was found dead in his apartment this morning. They're ruling it as a suicide, but I know better. It was only a matter of time before they came after us."

A chill swept through Bexley's core. As badly as she wanted to comfort him, she wanted to drag him down to the station even more to make him tell Grayson everything. "Who are 'they', Brewer? What are you running from?" When he didn't answer, she dug her fingernails into the palms of her hands. "I know about the obscene amount of money you're hiding. I know about the hospital bills for someone named Isabella, and donations to foster care."

He grunted with a humorless laugh. "You've been busy."

"I know you were running from something even before Mexico happened."

"Colt told me you suspected something was up." He took another drag of the cigarette, releasing a little at a time as he spoke. "I was hoping he could help with my predicament."

"When you say *predicament*, you mean trafficking cocaine?"

Jaw flexing, Brewer flicked the half-gone cigarette into the sand. "It's not what you think."

"That's good, because right now I'm thinking how I may never see the light of day again for aiding and abetting a drug lord. Why didn't you mention it earlier?" Her voice hitched when she asked, "How could you possibly believe it was something I didn't need to know?"

"I didn't think waking up in Mexico with a dead man would have anything to do with my past. I was convinced that part of my history was over with *years* ago. Then I got the call about Stinger this morning and heard about the warrant…it changed everything. Either way, I didn't want to get you involved. You were better off not knowing for your own safety. This shit is serious business. Someone's setting me up. I think they're trying to get the cartel's attention so I'll become their problem."

"Who would set you up? Who *are they*, Brewer?" she demanded in a firm tone.

He turned to her with a tight scowl. "It's complicated."

"I would hope it's complicated, otherwise I couldn't possibly understand why you'd ask for my help if you weren't going to be honest from the start."

He glanced down as his hands gripped his motorcycle jacket. "I've never lied to you."

"Hasn't it been established that omitting the truth and lying are the same thing?"

"I never wanted to be a criminal. I joined the Coast Guard because my birth mom O.D.'d on heroin two days after I was born. The docs said I was lucky she didn't appear to have used while she was pregnant, or I may not've survived. I figured I'd do my part to help keep that shit from crossing our border so it wouldn't happen to other kids."

Taking a deep breath, Bexley let the tension ease from her shoulders. "That's why you have a soft spot for kids in the system," she realized. "You were raised in foster care because your mom died."

She didn't suspect someone as noble as Brewer ever had bad intentions. She sensed somewhere along the way, something had broken him. Something had forced him to give up on everything he believed in, and take a wrong turn—one that landed him in a cheap motel, and kept him from engaging in meaningful relationships.

Gently setting her hand on his arm, she waited until he looked up at her. When he finally did, she could see the hurt he'd been trying to conceal. It lingered just beyond the surface of his gaze, consuming him.

"If you still want my help, it's imperative you tell me every last detail that might explain how those bricks of cocaine ended up in your storage unit. I can't possibly help you out of this situation unless you're straightforward with me. I want to know everything, from the beginning."

PART II

CHAPTER NINE

SAN PEDRO, CALIFORNIA

7 YEARS PRIOR

What Brewer Hawkins thought he'd always remember about his last day on duty with the Coast Guard was the way the love of his life looked at him that morning…like she couldn't wait for them to embark on a new adventure together. Pregnancy had made her more beautiful than ever. Her normally sharp cheek bones had filled out, and she'd taken on what he affectionately called her "mommy glow." Her jet black hair had grown several inches past her shoulders in a matter of weeks, and had taken on more of a natural wave. When her pretty little pink lips bent with a smile, her cheeks flushed and her swollen breasts heaved beneath the flimsy white nightgown she'd purchased when her other pajamas no longer fit.

Every day since, he'd wished he would've called in sick, or given *any* excuse not to leave her. Anything that would've stopped his worst nightmare from taking place.

"Good morning, gorgeous," Brewer whispered, taking her petite face in his large hands. He brushed his lips over hers in a soft, gentle kiss. She hated it when he kissed her before she had a chance to brush her teeth, but he savored any taste of her he could get. Sometimes it was the only thing that kept him going.

Before he could pull away she rolled to her side, wedging her swelling stomach between them, and deepening the kiss. Another advantage to her condition was the fact that she was in the mood for sex. All the damn time.

With a deep chuckle, he broke free from the suction of her mouth. "Baby, I can't believe I'm saying this, but I have to go. I'll have all the time in the world to give you what you want after today."

She released a low snort. "Yeah, except tomorrow the movers will be here, then we have two days to settle in the new place before my parents show up, and we'll be stuck with them as house guests for who knows *how* long. Maybe until Junior arrives."

"Wait," he said, his lips quirking with a grin. "You're calling our son *Junior* now? What happened to Matteo, and Gabriele, and whatever other weird-ass traditional names your mom's always going on about?"

She shrugged one sun-kissed shoulder. "I don't know…I've been thinking about it for awhile now, and I think Brewer Junior has a nice ring to it. Just because my parents are old fashioned and you don't know anything about your birth father doesn't mean we can't start new traditions of our own with our boy."

With a joyous holler, Brewer nudged her back onto her pillow and kissed her hard. He let the kiss evolve, deciding it was useless to deny her what she wanted. The moment he first laid eyes on the Italian knockout a year and a half prior, crying by herself on the beach with the news that her grand-mother had passed away on the other side of the world, he had a premonition that she could one day become the light of his life.

With time, he realized it wasn't only her smokin' hot body in a little purple bikini, or the way her beautiful smile made him forget they weren't alone on the beach that had him convinced. He'd never met anyone so full of positivity and compassion. She volunteered for half a dozen causes involving animals and senior citizens, and was working even more paid jobs so she could one day afford a degree in child education.

The night they sat in her apartment bathroom, and waited for the home test to confirm she was pregnant, Brewer knew there'd never be another woman in his life. He bent down with one knee on her tiled floor, and proposed without giving it a second thought. The next day, he started the process of transferring his GI benefits to her as an engagement present. He didn't want her to worry about how she'd afford college.

He'd had a good run with the military, and he doubted he would've survived without it. His foster father may've beat him to death if enlisting early hadn't been an option. But ever since he'd met the raven-haired beauty on the beach, he knew it was time to move on and start the kind of life he'd dreamed of as a kid—a stable home that was filled with happiness and love.

After they made gentle love that morning, Brewer showered and shaved before putting on his operational dress blues one last time. As always, there was a warm breakfast waiting for him when he was done. Considering how much time he'd lost attending to his fiancée's needs, he barely had time to scarf it all down before it was time to make the ten minute drive to base.

Before heading out the door, he pulled her close. "Don't forget to lock the door behind me."

"Is it really necessary to remind me that every single morning?"

Ignoring her, he lowered to his knees and nudged her cotton top upward. "I love you, Junior Hawkins." He kissed her round belly, pulling a happy little moan from her throat. "Be a good boy for your momma today. Don't be kicking her kidneys and giving her heartburn."

She bent to kiss the top of his head before helping him back to his feet. "You're already the best daddy in the world," she said, curling her fingers beneath his impeccably ironed collar. "And an insanely *handsome* one in this uniform. Have to say I'm going to miss seeing you decked out like this." Standing on her toes, she brushed her lips over his. "I love you madly, Brewer Hawkins."

He took his son's beautiful mother in his arms, wondering how he got so damn lucky. His entire body glowed with joy when he grinned down on her. "I love you more than life itself, Isabella Romano."

For as long as he lived, he'd never forget how breathtakingly stunning she looked as she waved goodbye from the kitchen window.

CHAPTER TEN

From the moment Brewer parked on base, he was filled with an unsettled feeling that started long before his team was called to inspect a vessel suspected of nefarious activity. He was so engrossed in the inkling that he didn't detect his best friend creeping up behind him to smack the back of his head until he felt the sting of Mugsy's hand.

"You checked out already, Hawk?" Mugsy teased with a deep chuckle. "You still have a full day ahead of you, my man! *Semper Paratus!*"

"Always ready," Brewer repeated with far less enthusiasm.

Mugsy squared himself in front of Brewer, giving him a keen once over. They'd been inseparable since their second day of boot camp in Camp May, New Jersey. The Brooklyn native was a fast-talker, and helped Brewer out of a sticky situation that got them both *quarter-decked*—forced into strenuous exercises within the barracks. At times it was downright impossible to take his 5'3" friend seriously, because 90% of the time, Roberto "Mugsy" García was completely full of shit.

"What's the matter wit you? Izzy got you shoppin' for wedding shit again?"

Brewer nodded. "Yeah, and we picked out baby pink ties for our pussy groomsmen."

"You wouldn't dare!" Mugsy cried with a look of sheer panic.

"Just messin' with you, my man." With a barking laugh, Brewer smacked Mugsy back. Mugsy reeled on him, throwing Brewer in a headlock with the ease only a high school state champion wrestler could possess. He may've been short, but he was scrappy as hell, and had dominated as a heavyweight.

"Foreplay this early in the day?" a deep voice boomed from the doorway. "Thought you two would at least wait until Hawk checked out."

Brewer maneuvered out from Mugsy's grip as Redding entered the locker room.

"Just gettin' him warmed up for ya," Mugsy replied.

Otis Welder—or "Redding" as the guys affectionately nicknamed him because of his love of blues music—was a tall, lanky blonde kid who'd ventured off the family farm in small-town Iowa. They'd only met him six months back when he was assigned to their base. His deep voice and boyish charm made him a hit with the ladies whenever they hit the town as a crew, which was fortunately something that didn't seem to bother Isabella. Brewer wouldn't have been able to handle it if she'd been jealous, because it meant she didn't understand he wouldn't dream of giving any other woman the time of day as long as he had her.

Mugsy lifted his chin and scowled. "What're you doin' here, Redding? Thought you were off this week."

"Yeah I'm off," Redding replied with a snort. "Off *your mom*. She says 'hi' by the way."

"Wise guy," Mugsy grumbled, looking ready to throw punches.

Redding started for his locker. "Heard you ladies got called out for an inspection. Thought I'd come along."

Brewer exchanged a confused glance with Mugsy. "Since when do you do ride alongs?"

Mugsy licked his lips and all at once started fidgeting with his collar, eyes jumping around the room. "You sure that's a good idea, Redding?"

"It's Hawk's last day." Redding smacked Brewer's shoulder. "Wouldn't wanna miss it."

"Wouldn't wanna miss what?" Stinger asked as he joined them.

Brewer and Mugsy had taken Benjamin "Stinger" Springer under their wing when he first joined their team. The quiet kid from Virginia was an easy target two years prior…not so confident, and carrying around an extra forty pounds that he'd since lost once he started tagging along to the gym with Brewer and Mugsy. Within weeks of becoming buff, he'd met a girl he called "the love of his life," and planned to marry her once they turned twenty-one. He still took endless amounts of shit because of his obsession with comic book heroes and other crap Brewer knew nothing about, but at least he owned it.

"Mornin', Captain Dorkus," Redding sang, draping his arm over Stinger's shoulders. "Did your mom sign your permission slip so you could come play with the big boys today?"

"Always with the mom jokes," Mugsy snarled behind him.

Stinger pushed Redding away. "What're *you* doing here?"

Redding cackled in the cocky way that got on everyone's nerves. "Thought I'd tag along with you losers today. Maybe teach you a thing or two about how it's done."

As Brewer grabbed his helmet from his locker, he noticed Mugsy seemed on edge. His square jaw was firmly set, eyes steely. Beads of sweat lined his thick hairline when he slammed his locker door. No one who knew Redding really liked the guy, and Brewer was especially irritated that he was going out with them on his last watch.

But whatever was bothering Mugsy was something more complicated.

CHAPTER ELEVEN

As Brewer navigated the response boat back to base following the interdiction, he decided he couldn't have asked for a better last day of service. They'd recovered several thousand pounds of cocaine bricks from a single-engine vessel. Air support had transported the smugglers back to land while Brewer and his team had unloaded the drugs into the cutter.

It was the kind of successful day at sea that made Brewer glad he'd enlisted. As he started the hour-plus cruise back to base, he was just beginning to realize how much he'd miss it—especially the countless hours of sunshine and fresh air that came with the job.

At the hull, his three teammates engaged in

some sort of heated debate that involved strained necks and wild arm movements. Suddenly Mugsy was cocking his arm back, ready to knock Redding out. Stinger nudged his way in between, face dark red as he shouted at each of them.

Brewer quickly eased the throttle back to idle. "What's goin' on up there?" he hollered.

Redding spun around, a brick of cocaine in hand. "Just doin' a little business."

"What the hell are you doing?" Brewer demanded, pointing at the contraband. "Why didn't you turn that in with the others? Have you lost your damn mind?"

"This little guy is worth twenty K," Redding reminded him. Smirking, he wiggled his eyebrows. "Only takes the misplacement of a few to earn a good living on the side."

Mugsy and Stinger stood to the side, eyes cast downward. It was as if their consciences were heavy with guilt. *What the actual hell?*

"You're talking about skimming contraband and selling it?" Brewer barked, his voice dropping a whole octave. "You're insane."

Redding's smirk grew. "I'm not selling it, numbnuts. I'm just passing it along to other resources, and taking a forty percent cut."

"Forty percent sounds pretty specific," Brewer said. "Almost as if you've done that kind of thing before."

"You thought I bought my sixty-six 'Vette with a government paycheck?" Redding shook his head and released a belly-laugh. "Get with the program, Hawk. Half the guys on base are doin' it. No one told you before now because they all think you'd narc."

Heat ripped through Brewer's chest. Damn straight he'd turn their stupid asses in. He took pride in serving his country. "Then why tell me on my last day? Why not keep that information to yourself?"

"Because we're lookin' for a mule on the outside." Redding lifted his chin in Mugsy's direction. "Your boy thought you'd be interested in earning a little extra with the wedding and kid on the way."

Brewer felt a rush of betrayal when he sternly eyed his best friend. "You're into this shit too?"

Mugsy's chin dropped to his chest. "Someone had to pay for my nana's bills, Hawk. Nursing homes ain't exactly cheap."

"You've got to be shitting me," Brewer grumbled, lacing his hands over his helmet.

"Hawk—" Mugsy started.

Brewer slammed the throttle down, almost knocking the others off their feet. He watched Redding closely as the traitor placed a call on the satellite phone. *How could Brewer have been so blind to what was happening around him?*

For the remainder of the trip, neither Mugsy nor Stinger would look Brewer in the eye. After years of working side by side with them, his best friend and teammate had become total strangers in the blink of an eye.

As Brewer moored to the dock on base, he couldn't get out of there fast enough. Redding stormed after him into the locker room. "You gonna narc on us, Hawk?" he demanded. "Be the asshole who lands his entire team in the clinker?"

Eileen from administration entered, one eyebrow arched. "Hawk, there's a call for you in the front office." The way her narrowed gaze skipped between the two men, it seemed she sensed the tension between them. "I'm sorry, was I interrupting something?"

"No, we're done here," Brewer stated. He shot Redding a dark look before heading out after Eileen. Once they reached her desk, she passed him the handset.

"Yeah?" Brewer answered, still harboring anger over his team's betrayal.

"Brewer Hawkins?" a man's voice grunted.

"Yessir."

"This is Detective John Baker from P.S.P.D. You're going to want to come down to PS General right away."

Brewer immediately honed in on the uneasy feeling he'd had all day. Stomach clenched, he gritted his teeth and squeezed the handset. "Why? What's going on?"

"I'm sorry to have to tell you this, but your fiancée was brutally attacked." The detective paused, forcing out a harsh breath. "It...doesn't look good."

CHAPTER TWELVE

A young blonde behind the reception desk in Papaya Spring General's emergency room sat rigid when she spotted Brewer storming in her direction. One of her hands reached for a telephone while the other braced against the desk.

"Isabella Romano!" he shouted through the plexiglass, his fiancée's name blazing through his throat like acid. *"Where is she?"*

The nurse held a finger up as she muttered something into the handset. Brewer shoved off from the desk, and raked his fingers through the patch of short hair on top of his skull. Ever since receiving the detective's call, his heartbeat had throttled against his throat, and wouldn't ease up. Paired with the massive pain in his chest, he was convinced he'd have a heart attack.

Isabella was his everything. When the detective told him she'd been attacked, he'd dropped to his knees, unable to pull in a breath. Eileen couldn't get a response outta him, so she'd yelled out for help. When Mugsy came running in, Brewer snapped back to his senses and shoved his friend aside on his way out the door. He blew through several stop lights on his motorcycle, and went three times the legal speed.

If anything happened to Izzy—or, *god help him*— his *son…*

Hit with a violent wave of nausea, he bent over.

A rather serious looking man with a thick mustache approached Brewer. He wore a tweet sports jacket, and emitted body odor. "Mr. Hawkins? I'm Detective Baker."

Brewer clutched one of the man's pudgy arms. "Is she…" he wheezed, "…the baby…"

"Let's go somewhere more private," the man suggested, glancing around the packed room. People coughed and fussed all around them, but all Brewer heard was the wail of a small baby.

"Tell me now!" he demanded, gripping the detective harder. *"What the hell happened?"*

"We believe the perp entered the back door of your home without forceable entry," the detective told him. "Either Miss Romano, *your fiancée*, knew the perp and let him inside, or the door was unlocked." The man lowered his voice, eyes dark with sympathy. "I believe she was attacked while she was trying to escape. She suffered several blows to the back of her head with a metal weapon—possibly a hammer or a crowbar. The surgeon in charge said it's too early to assess the overall damages. She's in surgery now. They're trying to stop the bleeding around her brain. If she survives, they'll place her in a medically induced coma until the swelling of her brain has cleared."

A high-pitched buzz assaulted Brewer's ears, and the room slanted.

No.

Not his Isabella.

What kind of monster would attack a pregnant woman?

"What about the baby?" he whispered. He shook the man with all his might. *"What about my boy?"* he bellowed.

The detective solemnly shook his head. "I'm sorry, son. She miscarried before the first responders arrived."

A mournful sound wrenched from Brewer's chest.

ISABELLA REMAINED IN A COMA FOR THREE MONTHS. In that time, Brewer only left her side when forced out by her sister or parents. The day the doctors came to tell the family that they didn't believe she'd ever recover from her injuries, Brewer was physically removed from the premises by security.

"With patients in Isabella's situation who have suffered a severe head trauma, there's always a chance of recovery," the head doctor told Isabella's parents. "However, your daughter is not showing any signs of brain activity. Keeping her on life support at this stage may prove to be pointless. And there's the issue of expenses incurred…the bills can become astronomical."

That's when Brewer had charged at the doctor, telling him he was wrong, and security was called.

Brewer paced the sidewalk across from the hospital, burning through an entire pack of cigarettes. He wouldn't let them take his Isabella off life support even though the Romano family had already lost their house in foreclosure, and their immigration status was under question. He refused to quit on Isabella because he knew she'd never quit on him.

Once she was healed, they'd try for another child. One could never replace the son they lost, *his namesake*, but he'd try anything to fill the gaping hole in his chest that grew with every day that passed.

It was on him to come up with the money, and he needed far more than he'd make fixing cars in the civilian job he'd lined up before leaving the military.

While sucking on his last cigarette, he grabbed his phone from his back pocket, and dialed his closest friend.

"Hey, man," Mugsy answered in a mournful tone, "I'm glad you finally called. Hawk, I'm so sorry to hear about Izzy and the—"

"Tell Redding I'm in."

CHAPTER THIRTEEN

Long after the Romanos returned to Jersey, Brewer continued to visit his fiancée every single day for hours on end. He didn't know what else to do with himself. He couldn't sleep, and had no desire to eat. He couldn't fathom going to work every day while Isabella fought for her life. Her attacker was still out there somewhere, and Detective Baker didn't have a single lead.

Despite her parents' wishes to let her go and honor her request to have her organs donated, Brewer refused to allow his beloved Isabella to be sliced apart that way. Not when she could still come back to him. The hospital staff treated him with kid-gloves, like he'd gone insane. Some days he wasn't so sure he hadn't.

The thing was, he'd been raised in a system that shuffled him from one abusive foster home to another, and he never understood the real meaning of love until he met Isabella. He couldn't imagine a reason to go on without her. There was no one else who mattered that way. He'd do anything to keep her around, and he did.

The drug gig was pretty simple. Whenever a bust was made, Brewer would meet up with one of his still active team members at a set location downtown just after sunset. He'd deliver the package the next day to an open locker at the bus station, closing it with a new padlock. Then he'd mail the padlock key to a "Fred Cannon" at a **PO Box** in L.A. with the locker number scribbled on the back of the envelope.

As many times as he assured himself he was only doing it for Isabella, the guilt for betraying everything he believed in—including his prior involvement in the military—started to fester. He punished himself by never indulging in a single damn thing, from a meal out, to a comfortable place to live. He didn't have the heart to move into the new house without Isabella anyway.

He took shelter under bridges, benches, public beaches—wherever he could sleep until he was chased away and had to find somewhere new. He'd run away from foster care enough times as a kid to know what it took to survive on the streets. He ate just enough to sustain his body, still losing all muscle mass and an extra twenty pounds. Whenever he saw a reflection of himself, he'd do a double-take.

He dutifully continued to play the part of a drug mule until eight months later when Isabella's parents secured a court order to terminate life support. Brewer had mourned his fiancée so many times that he was completely numb when watching the nurses end her life. He continued to sit in her room long after they'd wheeled her away to harvest her organs. For the last time, he was forcibly removed by security.

That night he drank his weight in alcohol, and woke curled on a bench ten blocks away from the bar where he'd started. The bender continued for weeks on end, allowing him to evade all contact with Redding and the other impure Coasties.

Two months after Isabella's funeral, he'd hit rock bottom. He didn't realize how far he'd fallen until Mugsy happened to walk by the pier where Brewer had been squatting.

"Hawk?" his friend gasped. "Oh shit, man, is that really you?"

At ten in the morning, Brewer had already polished off a 12-pack of cheap beer. He was coherent enough to recognize Mugsy's voice, and knew he had to get the hell outta there. There was no way he'd let his old friend see him that way. He reached over to scoop his bag from the sand, and fell on his side.

"Holy hell," Mugsy muttered, hooking Brewer by the arm, and dragging him back up to his side. "Brother, you're a mess, but it's good to see you. Everyone's been wonderin' what happened to ya."

"I'm done with Redding," Brewer mumbled, shaking his head. "I'm out."

Mugsy clapped Brewer's shoulder. "We *all* are. Stinger and me quit after you went missing. We were worried Redding or whoever he answers to had done something to make you disappear. You scared us, man."

It was the wake up call Brewer didn't know he needed.

Mugsy became a constant companion for the next few months, encouraging Brewer every step of the way to quit drinking, and get his life back on track. What remained of Brewer's share of drug money was donated to kids who were stuck in the system like he'd once been. He landed a decent job at an auto repair shop down the street from the motel where he'd been staying since becoming clean. A couple of years later, he started the paperwork to open his own shop, using what remained of his government paychecks.

He truly believed he had left his mistakes in the past.

PART III

CHAPTER FOURTEEN

PAPAYA SPRINGS, CALIFORNIA

OCTOBER 27TH

"For six years, I thought I'd never see Redding again," Brewer finished, letting out a weighted sigh.

Bexley remained mute on their perch atop the quiet bluff overlooking the city. The sun had long since slipped beneath the horizon, and thousands of lights in Papaya Springs twinkled with the false illusion of merriment. The last time she'd fought the need to shed tears, *real* tears that involved a snotty nose and chest-wrenching sobs, was…she didn't even know. Maybe at her mother's funeral.

Brewer's jaded past suddenly put everything into context. It was the reason he lived in the motel, and didn't seem to own any valuable possessions other than his motorcycle. It was the reason he only seemed to have meaningless flings, and showed no interest in commitment.

He was punishing himself.

Just when he thought he had the family he'd always wanted, he'd lost his child and the love of his life at the hands of an unknown murderer. The tragedy had triggered a bout of temporary insanity, causing him to partake in something that went against everything he believed in.

A lit cigarette dangled from Brewer's fingertips as he took a swig from the bottle of whiskey that Bexley had purchased at the convenience store down the road. "Don't waste your pity on me, Squires. I made the choices that led me down this path."

Bexley swallowed against the sorrow building in her throat. She understood the feeling of not wanting to be coddled. She also understood how lonely life could be without a supportive family. She'd always had Cineste, but even their relation-ship was strained for a time after Bexley ran off to New York.

"Life sometimes has a way of turning every-thing you know upside down," she said, wrapping her arms around her knees. Tilting her head his way, she sighed. She wished she could tell him she was sorry for everything he'd been through, as it sounded dreadful. But she knew it would only irritate him. "Are you aware that the detective who worked on Isabella's case is now Grayson's lieutenant?"

"Small world," he bit out.

"So this friend, Stinger…you think his death is related to Redding's operation?"

With a stony expression, he bobbed his head. "I suppose everyone's secretly fighting their own demons, but Stinger was a happy-go-lucky kind of guy. Never let much bring him down. He was always trying to bring everyone else up. Last time I talked to him was a few months back, and he'd just gotten married…they were trying to start a family."

Bexley's heartstrings tugged with the sorrow in his voice. "Have you kept in touch with Mugsy and Redding?"

"I haven't had anything to do with Redding since Izzy died. Mugsy reaches out every now and then to make sure I'm still on the straight and narrow. He's the one who told me about Stinger. He was a total wreck when he called."

"You still don't have any idea who was on the receiving end of the drugs?"

"No…but I have a feeling Mugsy knows something the way he was going on about how we need to get far away from Papaya Springs before we're next. He told me they have 'more disciples in this city than Jesus'. A lot of the other stuff he said didn't really make sense." Brewer inhaled a long drag before meeting Bexley's gaze. "I think he's losing his shit."

Bexley scrambled to her feet, and offered Brewer her hand. "Sounds like it's past time for the two of you to get reacquainted."

———

THE ADDRESS ROBERTO "MUGSY" GARCÍA HAD given to Brewer over a year prior brought them to a duplex not too far down the road from the Paxton siblings. The respectable community was lit with charming street lights, otherwise the majority of the homes remained dark. Most everyone would be in bed by that hour, resting up for another day of serving the city's finest. Once Bexley rang the doorbell of Mugsy's unit, a deep bark from inside was multiplied by neighborhood dogs. Seconds later,

Bexley was staring into the red-rimmed eyes of a beefy Hispanic man dressed in gym shorts and a sleeveless T-shirt bearing the Coast Guard logo.

The man grasped the studded collar of an agitated, brindle-colored American Staffordshire Terrier that drooled with every sharp bark. The living area behind him was in even more disarray than Simone's apartment had been. From the stench that came with dozens of empty beer cans and crumpled packs of cigarettes, Bexley guessed he'd been holed up in the duplex for days—perhaps even weeks.

"Who're you?" Mugsy snarled, reaching for the bulge of a weapon tucked into his waistband.

Bexley held her hand up to show him she was unarmed. "Hold on. I'm—"

Brewer stepped out of the shadows at her side. He held a protective arm out, shielding Bexley. "Relax, brother. She's with me."

Mugsy dropped his arm. "Hawk? You must be outta your mind comin' here! What if you were followed?" He leaned forward, eyes darting around the noiseless street. "Get your ass inside!"

Grabbing Bexley's hand, Brewer slipped in past his buddy. "We were careful," he assured Mugsy. "No one's following us."

With the door shut behind them, Mugsy commanded his dog to lay down. The beautiful canine licked his owner's hand before curling onto a worn pillow. Mugsy's suspicious expression traveled down to where Brewer had locked his fingers with Bexley's. "Glad to see you've finally moved on." A little smirk played on his lips as his gaze traveled up Bexley's skinny jeans, across her black and white striped tunic, and settling on her face. "You always had a thing for the hot ones."

The man's assumption and Brewer's failure to set his friend straight made it hard for Bexley to breathe. She felt an even stronger bond to Brewer after he'd shared his painful past with her, but she wasn't ready to act on anything.

"I'm a *private investigator*," she snapped. Before she was able to wiggle her fingers free, Brewer's hand tightened around hers. She added, "We're hoping you can help us fill in some of the blanks."

"I don't know nothin'," Mugsy replied, eyes narrowed on Brewer. "What'd you tell her?"

"Nothing she'll repeat," Brewer said with a shake of his head. "You can trust her."

"Who's behind the drug deals, Mugsy?" Bexley pressed. "Who did Redding answer to?"

Mugsy began to pace his tiled entryway, fingers

laced through his short, dark hair. "You don't understand. They're probably camped outside this place right this second, ready to take me out! To take *all of us* out!"

"No one's outside," Bexley insisted. "We swept the neighborhood before knocking on your door."

Brewer stepped forward, aligning himself nose-to-nose with his friend. "If you don't help us stop them, one of us might end up like Stinger. You ready to live with my death on your conscience?"

Mugsy balked, then stumbled backward a few steps. He tried to catch himself on the wall, but started going down. Brewer steadied him on his feet before he hit the floor, saying, "Whoa, brother. Take it easy." Then Brewer accompanied him into the living room, helping Mugsy lower himself to a clean section on the leather couch.

From Mugsy's clumsy, delayed reaction and enlarged pupils, Bexley worried he was high on something stronger than weed. It would explain his heightened state of paranoia.

Bexley cleared a spot on the end table across from Mugsy, and perched on the edge. "I want to put an end to this before either you or Brewer gets hurt. Tell us what you know."

"I don't know any names," Mugsy whispered,

head hung low. "I just remember Redding saying somethin' one time about gettin' to meet them in person once they decided he could be trusted. I saw him a few days afterwards…he was real spooked, said we had to mind our P's and Q's because there was nowhere safe to hide from them in Papaya Springs. He was real paranoid from that point on. When Stinger and me told him we were out a couple'a weeks later, he shook his head real sad like, said we were on our own."

"Do you know where he met with them?" Bexley prodded.

Mugsy shook his head. "He didn't say."

Bexley threw Brewer a skeptical glance. "Why would they come after you now, after years of radio silence?"

"Bet Redding knows," Mugsy gruffly answered. "He called me up one day last week outta the blue, sounded real jumpy. Wanted to know if I'd been talkin' to Hawk or Stinger recently. Said to call him if I heard or saw anything out of the ordinary. When I tried to get him to open up a little more, he hung up." He scrubbed his fists over his eyes. "I'm sorry I ever got involved in this shit."

Sounds like Redding deserves a visit next, Bexley decided. She gripped Mugsy's knee, waiting until his eyes fixed on hers. "Do you know where we can find him?"

Eyes glistening, Mugsy nodded. "He's staying in one of those ridiculous mansions out past Highland Avenue." He turned to Brewer. "It's the same place he'd always go on and on about back in the day. You remember the one?"

Brewer nodded. "Yeah, I remember." He turned to meet Bexley's curious look. "It was owned by that actor...the psycho that killed all those women."

***

Bexley was unable to shake the queasy sensation that followed her all the way from Mugsy's place on the east side of Papaya Springs to a cheap, off-the-beaten-path motel in downtown L.A. It seemed inevitable that she'd have to return to Dean Halliwell's home—the place where she'd almost become his last victim. The thought shook her to the core.

Since Colt Sawyer had towed Brewer's motor-cycle to the MC for safe keeping, Brewer waited in Bexley's SUV while she paid cash for a smoking room at the front desk. Although Bexley fully intended to drive back to her apartment after Brewer was settled in for the night, she didn't have the willpower to turn down the swigs of whiskey he offered.

As she sprawled out on the edge of the king bed, Brewer sat back against the quilted headboard, eyeing her while lighting a cigarette. He'd removed his shirt and settled in for the night, displaying his fit torso covered in fascinating artwork. The booze did nothing to fight her growing attraction to him. She was consumed by a warm rush filling her from head to toe.

"You're awfully thirsty tonight, Squires," he commented, his voice laced with sarcasm. "What's on your mind?"

Eyes closed, she stifled a snort. "I promise you, you don't want to know."

She heard him inhaling his cigarette, then slowly blowing the smoke back out. "For what it's worth, I regret getting you involved. I never would've asked for your help if I'd known the kind of danger I'd be putting you in."

"It's nothing new," she muttered. "Some jobs come with four-oh-one k plans. Mine comes with a valid reason to update my Will."

He released a deliciously deep chuckle. "I like

the way you always make me laugh. You're almost able to make me forget about all the dark shit I've been through."

"Life is funny that way." Flipping her eyes open, she rolled on her side to face him. She'd been kidnapped and framed for murder, but she was still most affected by the three seconds she entertained becoming romantically involved with a serial killer. "You can tell yourself a thousand times that you're okay, but it's never easy to make the darkness disappear."

He leaned over to extinguish the cigarette on an ashtray on the nearby nightstand. Then he lifted the bottle of whiskey, and his beautiful eyes darkened. "Com'ere."

"Oh no you don't," she sang, wagging a finger. She clumsily maneuvered around until she was sitting upright. "A bad boy tried to romance me once before. I mean, I realized it was a mistake before he was done kissing me, but it proved to be the worst moment of my entire life. That circus didn't end so well."

"What makes you think I'm a bad boy?" he asked, tilting his head. He sounded more amused than offended. "And why would that label matter? I could end up being the *best* thing that's ever happened in your lifetime. Between your job and the time we've hung out, you seem to enjoy living on the wild side."

Considering how right he was, she couldn't form a logical response to the contrary. The idea of letting herself explore a future with Brewer sparked something warm in the pit of her belly.

What if?

Before she could follow what was happening, he'd set the bottle down and moved to her side of the bed. As he slid his warm hand over hers, she could smell the nicotine on his breath, and feel the sporadic pounding of his heart in his fingertips. His bare chest radiated heat. An intoxicating blend of danger and excitement crackled in the air between them when she attempted to draw in her next breath.

"Does this have something to do with that detective?" he asked.

Her heart slammed to a standstill. She hated lying when it was so much easier to tell the truth. She thrived on making things less complicated. "Grayson and I were good together, you know?"

"Good's okay," he agreed, shrugging. "It's comfortable." His stare intensified. "But how do you know there isn't something better out there unless you give it a try?"

It was too much. Too soon.

While she believed Brewer's fiancée had been the driving force behind his unsavory actions, his story of not knowing how he ended up next to a dead body in Mexico hadn't been vindicated…yet. And she wasn't convinced she could be with someone who had intentionally broken a federal law. What would J.J. think of her if he knew about Brewer's past? Would he still entrust her to take over his legacy?

Desperate to make light of the moment, she rolled her eyes and let out a giggle that fell flat. The fiery way his enduring chestnut eyes watched her made it hard to think. "Aren't you the same guy who told me you don't do relationships?"

He seemed to be considering his answer carefully as his tongue slipped out to lick his lips, and his eyes darted to the corner of the room. "I once thought I'd never care for another woman the way I did for Izzy. But I learned as a Coastie that sometimes things happen beyond anyone's control, like when a tsunami capsizes a boat. There's no stopping it, no use in trying to fight. The only thing you can do is try to save yourself." Looking back down on her, his lips spread with a one-sided grin. "I'm starting to think you're my own personal tsunami." He leaned in a little closer. Close enough to kiss. "What do you say, Squires? Wanna ride the storm with me?"

The room spun and her heart throttled her ribcage. She wasn't sure if it was from the whiskey, or his suggestion. She gripped his wrist in an attempt to stay still. "I need time to process the events of these past few days. And I've had *way* too much to drink. Whiskey is not my friend. It's not even a close acquaintance. I might not remember a lick of this in the morning."

"Fair enough." His dimples sunk into his cheeks when he grinned. "If you forget anything about tonight, I'll be happy to give you a recap in the morning." With another delicious chuckle, he bent to kiss her forehead. She melted the second his warm, pillowy lips met her skin. "Good night, Squires."

Before her eyes closed, she remembered her head sinking into a cloud-like pillow, and a blanket being tucked beneath her chin.

CHAPTER FIFTEEN

Fire scorched Bexley's eyelids. Moaning, she threw an arm over her face and muttered, "Make it stop."

Her protest was answered with Brewer's deep laugh. "You weren't kidding when you said whiskey isn't your friend." The mattress buckled with his weight, and the aroma of dark roast wafted through the air. "I grabbed you a coffee from a cafe around the corner."

Little bits of memory from the night before returned. *Brewer had suggested they become involved, and she'd turned him down.*

Cheeks warming with a rush of embarrassment, she removed her arm. Brewer sat inches away, hair damp from a recent shower, white styrofoam cup in either hand, lips curved with a maddeningly sexy smirk.

She rose to her elbows, shaking her head. "Wait a minute. You *left* the motel? You remember you're hiding out because of a warrant and a possible hit on your life, right?"

"I wore the baseball cap you bought at the gas station. I made a point to go unnoticed." With another deep laugh, he held out the steaming coffee. "How much do *you* remember?"

She sat all the way upright, taking the warm cup and reveling in its delicious scent. "All of it," she confessed before taking a sip. When the liquid electrified her senses all at once, she hummed. "This tastes like the start of a successful day."

Brewer quirked an eyebrow. "Wanna talk about my idea some more?"

"Not now," she decided. A part of her wished she could merely disappear to avoid another meaningful conversation. "After I finish this cup, maybe I'll feel human enough to start surveillance on Redding's place. If he doesn't lead us to any suspects, I'll smoke him out and see what he knows."

Brewer pushed off the mattress and stood. "No need. Mugsy called me early this morning on the burner phone. Redding stopped by before the crack of dawn, said he was going to visit his mom in Iowa for a few days. He tried to convince Mugsy to go along."

"Sounds like Redding's even more spooked than Mugsy." Bexley ran her fingers through her tangled hair. "I'll find a way to confirm he's left. In the meantime, I have another case that needs my attention." She fished a few twenties out of her handbag on the floor, and tossed them on the nightstand. "Do us both a favor, and stay put this time. Order in when you get hungry."

"You expect me to stay *here* all day?" he grumbled, crossing his arms.

"Not really, but I wish you would." While starting for the bathroom, she threw him a sharp look. "I don't have the time or the resources to try to track you down if you go missing again."

LESS THAN HALF AN HOUR AFTER BEXLEY contacted Red with the request to track down Redding, the tech guru returned her call.

"I found a surveillance video that shows one Mr. Otis Welder boarding flight D-one-one-seven bound for Des Moines, Iowa, at six-fifteen this morning," Red reported. "Other than a rental car in Des Moines, activity on his credit cards is null. I'm assuming he's staying with friends or family since he hasn't made any deposits for a hotel."

"You tapped into TSA footage?" Steering through a residential neighborhood in Fullerton, Bexley shook her head. "Something tells me I don't want to know the lengths you go for these things."

Red added, "I feel I'd be amiss in my duties if I didn't tell you the guy looked sketchy as hell. I'm surprised they let him pass through security. Should we be notifying the authorities?"

"That's won't be necessary." Bexley parked in front of a well-maintained, tan and white bungalow at her GPS's direction. A sparkling pearl-white Cadillac sat in the driveway. "But do me a favor, and give me a call if anything more comes up under Brewer Hawkins's name."

Bexley ended the call before starting for the rambler. A white-haired elderly woman with a hunched back and deep wrinkles lining her narrow features appeared inside the front door. She greeted Bexley with a kind smile over sparkling white dentures. "You must be Miss Squires."

"Thank you for agreeing to meet with me on

such short notice, Mrs. Beers. I won't take much of your time."

The old woman waved a hand through the air. "It's not a bother. I welcome any visitors I can get. So often my days get to be painfully long with only my stubborn cat as company." Then she nudged the door open. "Won't you come in for a cup of tea?"

"I'm afraid I don't have—" Bexley began to reply. When the woman's expression turned hopeful, however, she changed her mind. Letting out a shallow breath, Bexley smiled. "Sure. I'd love to join you for a cup of tea."

The constant tick of a grandfather clock and a quiet meow from a hidden location were the only sounds to be heard as Bexley entered the residence behind Mrs. Beers. "Have a seat, dear. I'll put the kettle on the stove."

The pungent odor of moth balls and pine cleaner curdled Bexley's queasy stomach as she took a seat on a winged-back chair in a small living area. Based on the dark green wallpaper and thick shag carpet, Bexley guessed the house hadn't been decorated since the 1970s. Dozens of framed pictures lined the walls, many featuring a younger version of Mrs. Beers.

Curiously enough, the gallery included a recent

snapshot of Travis with Mrs. Beers. From the friendly way they stood with their arms around each other, posing beside the Cadillac in the driveway, it seemed their relationship went well beyond landlord/tenant. Mrs. Beers's eyes sparked with tears, and she beamed as if she'd won the lottery. *Curiouser and curiouser,* Bexley thought.

While waiting for the sound of the whistling teapot amidst the old woman's humming in the kitchen, Bexley mentally walked through Kiersten and Brewer's cases. If her suspicions were confirmed by Travis's landlord, Bexley would pay Simone another visit, hopefully catching the model alone. Bexley suspected that Simone didn't possess credible acting skills, and would expose her true feelings when Bexley suggested her brother's possible involvement in the heist.

While Bexley was relieved she wouldn't be making a trip to Halliwell's mansion in the near future, she realized that without having the ability to speak with Redding, she wasn't sure how she'd track down the drug kingpin. A trip to Iowa—as painful as it sounded—seemed unavoidable.

"Hope you like a good cuppa cinnamon," Mrs. Beers announced, waddling into the room with two steaming porcelain floral cups.

"Thank you," Bexley replied, accepting one. She took a tentative sip, surprised how much she enjoyed the dark liquid with a cinnamon kick. As Mrs. Beers settled into a gold arm chair, Bexley cleared her throat. "What can you tell me about Travis Paxton?"

The woman's face lit up with a smile. "Oh, he was a *lovely* tenant. Always paid his rent before it was due, kept the house immaculate, never had parties or played horrendous music." She folded her hands in her lap. "You know one time, on my eighty-seventh birthday, he brought me a large bouquet of red roses. It was almost as big as my kitchen table! Another time, he paid to have a team of gentleman landscape my yard. They put in a new sidewalk that goes all the way around the house, and filled in beautiful rocks around my prized lilac bushes." She leaned forward and lifted a hand to her mouth. "I'm not supposed to tell anyone this, but he even had a little fountain installed in the backyard featuring a sculpture of my late husband!" Leaning back, she laughed quietly. "That Travis has a big heart, I tell you. He's given me so many presents over the years, and he *insists* I don't have to worry about paying him back.

I was so sad to see him move away, but he promised he'd come back and visit me often."

So Travis hadn't been *evicted* as Simone believed, and he'd showered his landlord with extravagant gifts. With every second the woman spoke, Bexley was convinced the annoying stoner everyone else knew Travis to be was a carefully executed act. "Did he keep his promise to stop by for visits?"

Mrs. Beers nodded, her smile growing. "Oh yes. Every Tuesday evening after his afternoon shift, he brings me a fresh gourmet dinner from the restaurant. That boy can cook, I tell you."

"And does he still bring you presents? Like maybe that Caddy in the driveway?"

"The car was just one of many extravagant presents I've received. He's sent me on trips with my family, and paid off my mortgage." Tucking her chin, she flashed an adorably shy smile. "He makes me feel like Priscilla Presley."

Except Travis was no Elvis. "Mrs. Beers, are you aware if Travis works anywhere other than *La Belle's*?"

Once again, the woman cupped her hand around her mouth, eyes sparkling as if she was about to share a scandalous secret. "He sells a little bit of the marijuana on the side. He tells me it's perfectly legal because they can get it from stores now, but the rich college kids aren't all of legal age."

It would take a helluva lot of weed to pay for a new Caddy, Bexley decided. "Anything else?"

"Why are you asking so many questions?" The old woman's expression hardened. "Travis isn't in some sort of trouble, is he?"

"Oh no, it's nothing like that," Bexley lied. She set the teacup on the coffee table and stood. "I'm sorry to leave so soon, but I'm afraid I have other matters that require my attention."

"Come back anytime, my dear! I always welcome visitors!"

Even though she wasn't there for a social call, Bexley felt a twinge of guilt for leaving the old woman. Before starting her Explorer, she fired a text off to Grayson. She needed him to convince Craig Roth to reach out to his resources with a specific description of a perp. She included the picture she'd taken on her phone of Mrs. Beers with Travis beside the Caddy.

Bexley caught Simone as she was locking her apartment door. Despite the cool fall weather, the model wore a gauze white shirt over a scoop-cut bikini top the same color as her bubble gum pink nails, paired with torn jeans shorts. Her dog was tucked under one arm, and a beach bag under the other. Sensing Bexley before its owner, the dog yipped.

When the slender model whirled around, Bexley flashed a cheery smile. "Simone, hi! I was hoping you'd answer a couple more questions about the earrings."

"I don't have *time*," Simone snapped, slipping past Bexley. "I'm on my way to the beach."

Bexley jogged to keep up with the model's long strides. "I hope you packed a big blanket. Wouldn't want sand getting in all the wrong places during your tryst with Nick."

Gasping, Simone spun around. "How'd you know about us? Did he tell you?"

Satisfied with herself for being right about them, Bexley crossed her arms and smirked. "Unless the two of you were involved in the disappearance of the emerald earrings, I honestly don't care *what* you're doing in the sand." Then she threw Simone a stern look. "But I'll *only* promise not to tell his wife about his proclivity to young models if you'll answer my questions."

Simone's shoulders dropped. "I swear I didn't have anything to do with those earrings. I was just as surprised as everyone else. And I was dead serious when I said Nick isn't smart enough to pull something like that off. The man might be great in the sack, but there's not a lot going on upstairs. I'm only sleeping with him because I'm bored, and he's hot."

Rather than pointing out how Simone's "boredom" could break up a family, Bexley physically shook the annoyance from her head. "Is there any way your brother would've known about the earrings before the fashion show?"

"You think Travis stole them." From the tone of her voice and her even expression, Bexley wasn't sure how Simone felt about the accusation.

"Do you think it's possible?"

"Probably," Simone said with a shrug. "He can be super smart when he's not actively killing brain cells with weed."

"Did you maybe tell him about the earrings, or show him a picture?"

Simone dragged her bottom lip through her teeth while petting her dog's head. "I totally forgot until now…he took a picture of me wearing them. The day I went in for the initial fitting, he showed up early to give me a ride home. He said he was sending a snap of his hot sister to his friends."

Adrenaline spiked Bexley's core. *Her instincts had to be right.* "Where is he now?"

"He left for work, like, an hour ago."

Bexley darted back in the direction of the parking lot.

"Wait!" Simone called after her. "Are you going to arrest Trav because of what I said?"

Before Bexley reached her SUV, her phone pinged with a reply text.

Roth's contact made a positive ID on Travis Paxton
   He's our guy, Bex

ON HER WAY TO LA BELLE'S, BEXLEY CALLED Brewer. He answered the burner phone with a deep, grunted, "What?" It was hard to say if he was tired, or merely irritated from being caged up.

"I'm going to confront Redding in Iowa."

"He won't talk to you unless I'm there."

She'd begun to suspect Brewer would insist on coming along. Still, he was a wanted man. "How's that going to work? You won't last five minutes in the airport before you're arrested, and it's an entire day's drive. We don't have that kind of time."

"Give me a couple hours. I can easily get my hands on a new ID, and we'll be on our way."

"Are you sure you want to risk it?"

"I need to know who had Stinger killed."

It was a dangerous confession—one that implied consequences would follow—but Bexley understood where he was coming from. And she was grateful he wasn't joining her because he was worried about her safety.

La Belle's parking lot was packed, forcing Bexley to park in the alley behind the restaurant. Heidi Steele, the waitress who had found Temperance's dog after it'd been kidnapped, just happened to be smoking a cigarette by the back door.

Heidi let out a high giggle as Bexley started for her. "Should'a known I'd be seeing you again."

"How have you been, Heidi?" Bexley asked, stopping a few feet away. "How's your daughter?"

The lanky brunette stretched her arms out at her sides. "As you can see I'm still livin' the dream. I had to take on more shifts after I kicked Davis out." She sucked on the cigarette, momentarily deep in thought. "The last time he knocked me around, his fist missed the baby by an inch. I decided Casey couldn't grow up in a home like that."

"That must've been hard," Bexley told her, relieved to hear she'd taken a stand. Maybe there'd be hope for little Casey to grow up in a safe environment.

Heidi didn't say anything as she tossed the cigarette onto the concrete, stomping it out with a worn ballet flat. "I suppose you're here to see Travis."

"Can you get him for me?"

"No can do. He up and quit about a half an hour ago. Didn't give a notice *or* explanation. Just gave me a hug and told me to take good care of myself and Casey."

Simone must've given him a heads up. "Do you know where he was headed?"

"No, but I have something for you." Heidi pulled a sealed white envelope out from her pants pocket. "He told me to give this to the hot detective lady that would come around asking questions about him. I should've figured it'd be you."

Bexley took the envelope. "Thanks, Heidi. Take care."

Once she was back inside her SUV, she eagerly tore the envelope open.

Dear hot detective lady,

Though I'm impressed by your adroitness, you're still a day too late and a dollar too short.

You forced me to split town earlier than planned.

No one in Papaya Springs would move the earrings once you started sniffing around, so I suppose the $5M I've already swindled will have to suffice.

I left the earrings at my sister's. They're underneath the couch cushions (she never cleans the place). I figured you seem nice enough, so I wanted to help you by placing another solved case under your belt.

Simone was 100% uninvolved in the heist. She's really as dense as she appears. No need to drag her into my shenanigans. Between our shitty parents and a string of old men using her, she's been through enough.

Don't waste your valuable time looking for me. Once you came around, I decided to get my affairs in order, and prepared a foolproof plan to flee the country if you were to get too close. I'm off to live the kind of footloose and fancy-free life I've dreamed of for as long as I can remember. One that's filled with adventure, love, and unbridled happiness. I'm done with this work-yourself-to-an-early-grave bullshit this country has drilled into our heads.

As Socrates once said, "It is not living that matters, but living rightly."

I hope you do the same.

A slow smile crept across Bexley's face. Though she would've preferred to put someone behind bars for the theft, she couldn't help but feel satisfied. His confession lifted the heavy weight from her conscience. Not only would she be able to return the earrings to Kiersten, essentially saving her best friend's career, but her time was freed up for a trip out of state.

CHAPTER SIXTEEN

By the time the golden crop fields of rural Iowa rolled past, sunrise peaking in beautiful pastel tones across the horizon, Bexley was grateful for the sleep she'd caught on the flight over. She'd never seen a highway as quiet as the one that led them to Otis Welder's family acreage, and it was imperative that she stay alert. Several times she was forced to slow down for enormous machines that took up three quarters of the asphalt. She knew the alternating green and red monstrosities must be used for some type of farming purpose, but couldn't imagine what was involved.

While Brewer secured a false identification, Bexley retrieved the earrings from Simone and returned them to Kiersten. Both women were moved to tears with the news. Simone was certain Bexley was going to call the police and have her arrested. Kiersten was so excited to have the genuine emeralds back in her possession that she'd been on the verge of passing out.

Because of the trip to Iowa, Bexley refused Kiersten's offer to take her out for dinner "somewhere fabulous" to celebrate. Instead Bexley reluctantly agreed to Kiersten's second offer that involved ridiculously frivolous activities like massages and manicures the following weekend.

Bexley reached out to Grayson next, wanting to thank him for all he'd done, but the call went straight to his voicemail. He'd never rejected her calls before, and she wasn't quite sure how it made her feel.

With a handful of miles to go, Brewer stirred awake in the compact car's passenger seat, rubbing both hands over his face. Bexley agreed it was necessary to alter his appearance, but she doubted she'd ever adjust to seeing him clean-shaven with uniformly short hair. His lips were fuller, jaw thicker. Even his eyes suddenly seemed a clearer hue of chestnut brown, and their golden flecks danced. The stroke of a razor had amplified everything that made him attractive. It felt as if a stranger was sitting beside her. Most eerie was the way he'd covered his inked skin with a concealer—an idea he copied from an ex-girlfriend who taught at a strict daycare—and wore a chambray button-down. Bexley had never seen him appear so… straight-laced. He could've passed for an investment banker or lawyer.

It irritated Bexley to no end the way the new look completely stole her ability to breathe. Especially when she actually missed his tattoos.

"Stop looking at me like that, Squires," he grumbled behind his hands. "I'm self-conscious enough already. I've never felt so damn naked."

Pretending she hadn't heard him say "naked" and that it hadn't invoked an interesting visual, her eyes snapped back to the road. "You've missed out on all the fun. I've been playing Frogger with farm equipment the size of houses for the past hour."

He removed his hands from his face and arched a single eyebrow. "Why does it suddenly feel like we're on the set of a horror movie?"

She loved that his mind went to the same dark place. "That would explain all the chainsaw wielding psychos and possessed children I've passed."

With a chuckle, he motioned to her phone

perched on the dashboard. "Looks like we're almost there. I should be able to charm my way inside without any problem. The time Redding's mom came out to visit us on base, she thought I was the best thing since sliced bread."

At the intersection, Bexley glanced over her left shoulder for oncoming traffic, and rolled her eyes to herself. "Don't you mean the best thing since catnip was introduced to cougars?"

"You afraid of losing me to an older woman, Squires?" Brewer teased.

Too afraid of where the banter would lead, Bexley let the jab slide. GPS took them to a long driveway flanked with dried cornstalks twice as tall as the rental car. Bexley was certain the app was leading them to their untimely death until a grand, two-story farmhouse came into view. It was surrounded by barren fenced-in pastures and dilapidated buildings.

A remodel had begun on the 18th century structure in which they'd started to add a Craftsman-style porch with exposed beams. Yet it was only partially complete, and there weren't any tools or materials nearby to indicate the presence of a contractor.

"Redding's dad died a few years back," Brewer

commented bitterly. "You'd think he'd have the decency to use his drug money to hire someone to finish this place."

Bexley parked beside the only vehicle in the yard—a white sedan with Florida plates and a barcode at the base of the windshield.

"Must be his rental," she said. "Hopefully that means he's here."

"It's early enough…he'll probably still be in bed." Reaching for the door handle, Brewer glanced at her over his shoulder. "Follow my lead."

Slightly annoyed that he assumed he was in control of the situation, Bexley grumbled to herself as she grabbed her handbag and stepped out of the car. In a stark comparison to California, it was crisp outside—enough that she could see her breath, and she wished she'd brought more than her lightweight moto jacket. Huffing on her chilled hands, she met up with Brewer beneath the partially constructed porch when he rang the doorbell. As the ornate blue door began to swing open a few moments later, he slipped his arm around Bexley's shoulders and pulled her close.

A curvy, attractive woman in her mid-forties scowled back at them. She wore an oversized "Highly Suspect" band t-shirt over bare legs and tattooed arms. Her dark hair hung in tangled waves down to where her free nipples pressed against the thin cotton. "Can I help you?"

"It's me, Nic," Brewer replied with a deep chuckle, "Brewer Hawkins. I know it's been a few years, but—"

"Oh my god, Hawk!" the woman squealed, pouncing on him with open arms. "It's been *ages!* I'm so glad you're here! Something's not right with my O-man!"

Bexley attempted to pull away from the awkward ambush, but Brewer's strong hand slipped down to lock around her waist as he withdrew from the woman. "That's why I came," he lied, flashing one of his irresistible grins. "I figured he needed a friend."

"Oh, Hawk, you always were so sweet…and so *handsome.*" She ran her hand down his muscular arm, then threw Bexley a terse smile. "Who's your friend?"

"My *girl*-friend," he corrected with an air of pride, squeezing Bexley against him. "Bexley, this is Redding's mom, Nicole."

Girlfriend? Bexley would find a way to make him pay for the little charade. In the meantime, she'd play along. "It's so nice to meet you, Nicole," she told the woman, injecting honey into her voice. "Brewer had nothing but sweet things to say the time he met you in California."

Nicole's smile warmed until it felt genuine. "Well, you got lucky with this one, Bexley. He's the total package." While throwing Brewer a sultry wink, she took a step back, holding the door open. "Come in! I'll get breakfast going while you wake O. He's in the last room on the right up on the second floor. He'll be so surprised to see you here!"

She has no idea, Bexley thought as she stepped over the threshold with Brewer, praying Redding's paranoia hadn't provoked him into sleeping with a gun.

The interior of the farmhouse was a sharp contrast from the outside. They deposited their shoes into a pile by the door and left Nicole in the industrial kitchen, wandering into a living room filled with pristine, modern-style furniture and newly engineered wood floors. Black and white murals of different rock bands in concert plastered several walls, and each room featured subtle decorations in hues of blue. On their way to the open stairway, they walked past an impressive grand piano and an acoustic guitar. The faint odor of weed clung to the air.

"Maybe Redding has been good to his mom after all," Brewer whispered to Bexley.

She shivered when his warm breath tickled her ear. After removing his boots he'd claimed her hand, and she really hoped it was part of the act. "We need to be on high alert," she whispered back. "He might not like the fact that you're in his home after six years of radio silence."

"I'm not scared of him," Brewer said with a chuckle.

"Maybe you should be."

The wooden treads creaked and groaned beneath each of their footsteps. The second floor hadn't been updated like the main level. The hallway was in dire need of paint and new carpet. And it was unusually dark, conjuring more visuals from horror movies.

Bexley's heartbeat thrummed in her chest as they neared Redding's door. She suddenly doubted herself for traveling all that way to confront a man who was afraid and on the run.

But Brewer didn't allow her any more time to dwell on her decision. In a blur, he stormed into the room filled with trophies, and plucked a scruffy blonde man from a queen bed by fisting the front of his t-shirt.

Redding's eyes popped open and his jaw dropped. The men were nearly equal in height, but Brewer was muscular everywhere while Redding was skin and bones. He was no match for Brewer.

"Hawk? Wha—"

With one well-placed punch, Brewer knocked him down to the floor with a loud thud. *"Who were we working for?"* Brewer bellowed. *"Who killed Stinger?"*

The sudden burst of anger unnerved Bexley. As she tried to formulate a plan to intervene, she heard Nicole charging up the stairway, calling her son's name.

"Brewer, his mom's coming," Bexley warned.

Again, Brewer grabbed Redding by his t-shirt, this time helping him back to his feet. "Pretend nothing's wrong, and I won't tell your mom you're a lowlife drug dealer."

Redding jerked his shirt from Brewer's fist, chin held high, eyes hard. It's was anyone's guess whether or not he'd go along with the idea.

"Otis!" Nicole panted as she entered the room. "Baby, are you alright?" She eyed the two men closely. "What the hell is going on up here?"

"He surprised me is all," Redding replied. His eyes traveled down to her t-shirt. "Put some damn clothes on, woman! *No one* should see you dressed like that!"

His mom's mouth twisted with an unsatisfied scowl as she crossed her arms over her breasts. "Are you sure you're okay?"

"Yes!" Redding snapped. "Now please, for the love of God, put something decent on—starting with a bra!"

"Stop being so dramatic around our guests. Breakfast will be ready in fifteen." Nicole rolled her eyes in Bexley's direction and giggled as she vacated the room.

Redding's eyes narrowed. "I thought you were dead, Hawk."

"Why, because you were told there was a hit out on him?" Bexley asked.

"Who're *you?*" Redding snarled back at her.

With a flick of her elbow, Bexley nudged the door shut. "I'm the private investigator Brewer hired to find out who planted cocaine in his storage unit," she snarled back. "I'm not leaving until you tell us who was on the receiving end of those drugs."

Redding released a high, nervous laugh. "You think I'm just going to give you a name, sweetheart?"

Brewer loomed over him, looking ready to throw another punch. "Stinger is *dead* and I'm pretty sure someone tried to kill me in Mexico. Mugsy told me they quit your fucked-up gig shortly after I did. Why would they come after us now, and not back then?"

"Because I recently tried to get out, okay!" Redding blurted. "Only they didn't take kindly to the idea of letting me go when I know too many of their secrets! I guess they saw the rest of you as more loose ends I was leaving behind!"

Head tilted, Brewer stared at Redding like he was trying to decide if the confession was truthful. "What do you mean you 'tried'?"

"Why?" Bexley pressed.

Redding turned toward a window overlooking one of the empty pastures. "I was recently given a promotion of sorts. A few weeks ago, I came across some information from the higher-ups about shit that went down…regarding the way they do business." His head hung lower as he continued to speak. "Smuggling drugs was relatively harmless—I wasn't hurting anyone. We all know junkies will find a way to get a fix whether it's through me or some other guy." He reached behind his head, grasping his neck. "But killing innocent people…making some their *slaves*…man, that's entirely different. I want nothing to do with that kind of bullshit." With a remorseful look, he turned back to Brewer. "I didn't think they'd come after you guys. You gotta believe me, Hawk."

"Tell us who 'they' are," Brewer told him. "If they're as powerful as you say, this won't end until they're behind bars."

"If I rat them out, they'll kill us both." He jerked his head at Bexley. "Her too."

"I won't let them anywhere *near* her," Brewer growled protectively, teeth barred.

Bexley patted Brewer's shoulder, barely resisting a "down boy." She lifted her chin at Redding. "What if we could get you into a witness protection program?"

His eyes rounded. "You could do that?"

"I know someone who could," she said, nodding. "This has to stop *somewhere*, Redding. If you don't, *who knows* how many more innocent people will die as long as they're in business. Can you really live a normal life with those deaths on your conscience? How long do you think you can run before they catch up with you?"

"I don't want to be on the run for the rest of my life," he admitted in a wavering voice. "And I don't want to see any more of my friends killed." Tears glistened in his eyes. "What if they come after my family next? My mom…my little sister?"

"Tell us who's trafficking the coke," Brewer said to him. "We'll make sure they're put away before they can hurt anyone else."

"Whoever you're running from is human just like the rest of us," Bexley added. "They *can* be brought down, no matter how powerful their delusions."

A deep sob tore from Redding's lips. "I'm sorry, Hawk! I had nothing to do with it! You have to believe me! I didn't know, man! I had no idea what they were planning! I never would've agreed to it!"

Brewer's eyes muddled with confusion. "Planning with me an' Stinger?"

"Not just that, man, I mean with—"

A loud ping pierced the air.

There was suddenly a spiderweb pattern in the window with a small hole in the middle.

Bexley and Brewer silently watched as Redding touched his shoulder.

It was bleeding.

How? Bexley wondered. *What's happening?*

Redding's face paled. "They're already here," he whispered.

"Get down!" Brewer roared, diving toward Bexley. He hooked his arm around her waist and slammed her down to the floor behind the bed with a hard *thump.* Bexley moaned as a sharp pain radiated through her bones.

Redding lowered down to their level, collapsing on his backside a mere second before another crack came from the window. That's when it registered with Bexley that someone was shooting at them. Her brain was trying to protect her by going into shock.

"How bad is it?" Redding asked, turning to Brewer. The bleeding had accelerated, covering his entire hand and saturating his white t-shirt.

Finally coming back to her senses, Bexley swiped a damp bath towel off the floor beside her. "Keep pressure on it," she told Brewer, placing the towel over Redding's wound. She reached for her cell phone inside her handbag. "I'm calling an ambulance."

"Forget it," Redding told her. "We can't get a signal out here. You have to use the landline in the kitchen downstairs. Mom wanted to get rid of the dumb thing, said it made her feel old, but I told her she had to keep it in case of emergencies." His complexion turned a ghastly white. "Oh shit. *Mom.*"

He tried getting up, but Brewer nudged him back down. "What if they shot her too?"

Bexley lightly squeezed his forearm. "I'll check on her—make sure she's alright."

"You stay here, I'll go," Brewer offered.

She shook her head. "Keep applying pressure to his wound. There's no chance of getting those names from him if he's dead." She produced her stun gun from her handbag. "I brought this in my checked bag, just in case. I'll be okay."

As Brewer held her gaze for a beat, Bexley felt something profound wash over her. It was a feeling that went well beyond protection.

"Be careful," he pleaded. "There could be more of them in the house."

She nodded in understanding. As she crawled toward the door, she was seized with an over-whelming urge to kiss Brewer. He'd let her go without putting up a fight. He truly believed she was capable of saving the day.

She hoped he was right.

CHAPTER SEVENTEEN

Bexley crept down the steps in her stockings, sliding her back against the wall and holding her thumb over the trigger on her stun gun. At the rate her heart was pumping blood and rushing through her ears, she was sure its thumping was audible. The bitter smell of charred bacon permeated the air, and smoke clung to the rafters. She could hear it sizzling among the lull of a rock ballad. How long until the fire detectors were triggered? Was Nicole merely a bad cook, and blissfully unaware someone was shooting at her house? Was she hiding? *Dead?*

With every step Bexley took closer to the kitchen, a crippling panic began to set in. She wasn't trained to dodge bullets, or take down a shooter. In fact, the last time someone had fired shots her way, she'd called Cineste's boyfriend to save her.

The tension in her chest unfurled a little once she located Redding's mom, who appeared physically unharmed. The woman cowered on the kitchen's white tiled floor beneath a row of windows, backside pressed to the lower cabinets, bare legs tucked against her chest, greasy spatula clutched in hand. Above her, three bullet holes pierced the windows, leaving a glittery trail of glass on the countertop.

It appeared Nicole was seized with fright. With the site of Bexley coming at her, however, her eyes went wild. Bexley held a finger to her lips as she lowered down to the floor and crawled to the stove, turning off the burner. Once she traveled the remaining distance to sit beside Nicole, it felt as if she'd been holding her breath ever since leaving Redding's room. She released it with a silent pant before turning to Nicole. "Are you okay?"

The woman's hazel eyes skipped down to Bexley's stun gun. "Did you and Hawk lead these animals to my home?"

Bexley grunted. "You'll have to ask *your son* why they're here."

Nicole's voice tightened when she asked, "Where *are* the boys?"

"Otis has been shot."

A whimper rose from Nicole's chest as she clasped her hands over her mouth.

"I'm convinced he's going to be okay," Bexley assured her, "but we need to call an ambulance. Where's the phone?"

With a trembling hand, Nicole pointed across the massive kitchen to a home office alcove. Among a laptop and large speakers, Bexley spotted the rotary phone. "Stay here," she told Nicole before crawling in that direction. Every second that passed when her knees and the palms of her hands hit the cold tile felt like a countdown to her execution. Once tucked away in the alcove, she blindly reached up to the desktop and felt around for the phone.

A man wearing a semi-transparent mask with holes for his eyes and mouth breached the kitchen entrance. He was dressed in all black from his stocking cap to his boots, and wielded a large pistol.

"On your feet," he demanded in a deep, gravelly voice while charging at Nicole.

"Please don't hurt me or my son!" she cried. As she reluctantly stood, Bexley realized the man hadn't noticed her crouched in the alcove behind him.

"Call your son and his friends!" the man barked. "Get them down here, now!"

Nicole raised her hands up to the ceiling. "Okay! Okay, I will!"

As Nicole called her son's name, Bexley gathered the courage to sneak up behind the man, stun gun aimed at his lower back. She hoped it contained enough wattage to bring the beefcake down. In the same moment she was ready to fire, the man's ears perked.

He spun around. Her heart slammed to a standstill as he raised the pistol.

"Hey, asshole!" Brewer yelled from the kitchen's threshold. "Get *the hell* away from her!"

The man's head snapped in the other direction, giving Bexley the perfect opportunity to apply the prongs to his jugular. He dropped to the floor with the finesse of a sack of potatoes.

The deafening sound of large tires spinning on gravel roared from outside. Nicole ran to the window. "We must've scared his friends away!"

Brewer rushed past Bexley, pushing his knee into the man's back and gathering his hands together. He glanced up at Nicole. "Do you have any rope or large zip ties lying around?"

"I think my husband kept some in the garage," she answered, dashing from the room.

Brewer's eyes shifted to where Bexley grabbed the house phone. His expression softened. "You alright?"

While dialing 9-1-1, she answered him with an affirmative smile.

THE ARRIVAL OF EMERGENCY PERSONNEL TO THE Welder acreage was chaotic. A firetruck arrived right before two ambulances. Minutes after that, the driveway filled with half a dozen local PD and sheriff cars with every last light flickering and siren wailing. Nicole was near hysterics once she saw how much blood Otis had lost, and began beating the shooter with a boot.

The man refused to reveal his identity. Once he was cleared by a set of paramedics, they quickly hauled him off in the back of a police car. Bexley was busy watching the other paramedics load Redding into the ambulance, and lost track of Brewer in the mayhem.

A tall, fair-haired man wearing a sheriff's badge approached Bexley. "Miss Squires, I'd like you to come down to the municipal station for a thorough questioning." He motioned to a white vehicle with SONG COUNTY SHERIFF displayed in large black letters along the side. "You can follow my squad car into town."

Bexley balked when noticing *Brewer* was sitting in the caged backseat. From the awkward angle he leaned forward, she assumed his hands were cuffed behind him. "What's Brewer doing in there?" she demanded. "Where are you taking him?"

Glancing over his shoulder, the sheriff tipped his tan cowboy hat back. "Mr. Hawkins willingly provided his name, and informed us there's a warrant for his arrest in California. He wanted to go in peacefully."

Brewer caught her wide-eyed stare and smirked before mouthing the words, *"It's o-kay."*

"Take it easy on him," she told the sheriff. "Those absurd charges are directly connected to this shooting. He's being set up."

"That's for a court of law to decide, ma'am," he answered. "I'm merely doing my job of executin' the warrant."

Bexley climbed into her rental and followed the

entourage of law enforcement cars for ten miles into a little town. Aside from a few dozen simple houses—some appearing long since condemned—the only other buildings consisted of a chain variety store, and a chain gas station.

Local law enforcement appeared to be in over their heads with the shooting. Both sheriff deputies and local city officers filled the small building to its limits, buzzing around like bees in a hive while a chorus of phones rang on an endless loop. Bexley doubted the small, sleepy community had ever been forced to deal with any crime more extreme than a juvenile prank involving livestock and a staircase.

A young, eager-to-accommodate deputy named "Peck" instructed Bexley to wait in the municipal building's break room since their only interrogation room was already occupied. By the time she was questioned by the sheriff and half a dozen of his deputies, they decided her story matched the statements given by Nicole and Brewer, and told her she was free to leave.

But she wasn't going anywhere without Brewer.

Numerous calls to Grayson and Luke Jacobs went unreturned. She finally spoke with Luke's secretary to discover he was in trial, and wasn't expected to be available until early evening. Bexley practically bounced off the plain white walls as she waited to hear of Brewer's fate. Sometime early afternoon, Deputy Peck brought her a sub sandwich and chips with a bottle of water. She dozed shortly after that with her head propped on her arms over the table.

She woke to the sound of a sharp knock.

Her heart seized with the sight of Grayson stepping into the room wearing a crisp suit and tie. Although shocked by his presence—she hadn't left any details of her predicament in her voicemail—she was grateful to see him. They each grinned and silently met in the middle for a friendly embrace.

"This is starting to feel like *Groundhog's Day*," he quipped, squeezing her a little harder. "You spend more time in sheriff stations than your own office."

Laughter stuck in her throat as she drew back. "What are you doing here?"

"Lieutenant Baker sent me. I reached out to a few contacts on the flight over, and made arrangements for Welder once he's out of surgery. As long as he gives us names, we can promise his safety from that point forward."

"They think he's going to make it?" she hoped, gripping his arms.

"Sounds like it. They were able to stop the

bleeding, and the bullet didn't hit any major arteries or organs."

"How did your lieutenant know to send you? How'd you know about the deal?"

"Apparently your *friend* has some kind of history with Baker." Grayson's smile vanished. "He called the station and gave him the details of the deal you proposed to Welder."

"What's going to happen to Brewer?"

"He'll be extradited back to Papaya Springs. His fate will be in the hands of the new DA."

Dread climbed up her throat. "They appointed a new DA?"

"Mariah Holmes."

Flinching, Bexley released him. Holmes was the depraved assistant DA who had attempted to prosecute Bexley for a bogus murder fashioned by the Mayor and elected DA. If Brewer was going to have a chance in hell of fighting whatever charges Holmes was prepared to throw at him, Bexley needed to retain Luke on Brewer's behalf as soon as humanly possible.

Her gaze cut to where Deputy Peck stood in the doorway. "Can I see Brewer?"

"I'll see what I can do," he replied, nodding with a smile before wondering off.

Expression all at once stony, Grayson held out a plastic card. "I got you a room in the only motel nearby. Figured you'd want to clean up and stick around until I'm done with Welder. I'll be staying in the room right next door. If everything goes as planned, we can catch a flight home together mid-morning."

Although she had intended to head back to California once she was released, the idea of freshening up sounded more appealing. "Thank you," she said, taking the card and tucking it into her back jeans pocket. "I could sleep for days right about now." When he started for the door, she grabbed his hand and tugged him back. "I truly appreciate all you've done for me lately. Maybe we can grab a bite to eat later?"

Glancing down at the floor, Grayson straightened his tie. "I don't know—"

Deputy Peck returned in the doorway. "Sorry to interrupt. Miss Squires, the sheriff is allowing you ten minutes with Hawkins before they start transport."

Grayson turned his back on Bexley. "I'll let you know when I'm finished here."

With a helpless sigh, Bexley watched him leave. It was obvious her relationship with Brewer was hurting him, and she didn't know how to make it right.

———

SEEING BREWER LOCKED INSIDE A CRAMPED JAIL cell was beyond disheartening, but Bexley faked her way through it, greeting him with a crooked smile. "I can maybe learn to live with the clean face and short hair, but drab khaki is definitely not your color."

Chuckling, he rose from the cot and shuffled over to the bars, gripping them in his hands. "You've been here this whole time?"

"You thought I had something better to do?" A feeling of helplessness clutched Bexley's insides when she reached out to wrap her fingers over his. The connection both warmed her throughout, and made her sad at the same time. How long would it be until she'd see him again without a set of bars between them? "You may have saved my life today."

He smirked. "May have?"

"Okay," she rolled her eyes and clicked her tongue. "If you're going to play the hero card, I'm pretty sure you don't get to brag."

A deeper smile spread over his lips. "You were doing just fine on your own. I just helped you out with a little distraction." Suddenly taking on an intense look, he lightly stroked his index finger along hers, sending an army of shivers down her spine. "I'm just glad you're okay, Bex."

"I'm going to call Luke Jacobs the second I leave this ho-dunk station," she told him, watching as their fingers interlocked together around the bars. She hadn't intended to show him that sort of affection, but she was unable to stop herself from wanting more. "Don't waste your time picking out a prison nickname, or befriending the biggest guy in the yard, because by the time you reach California, he'll have formulated a defense to spring you free."

"Hey," Brewer drawled, "look at me."

Her eyes slowly traveled from his hands to his chest, taking their time studying his firm jaw and pillow-like lips, the angular slope of his nose. By the time she was staring into his beautiful brown eyes, she felt the burn of tears forming. Though it seemed childish, she couldn't help thinking it was unfair they'd be separated right when she'd finally decided it was time to look into a future of some type with Brewer Hawkins.

"Don't waste your energy *or money* on posting

bail, Bex. It's time I own up to the crimes I've committed…pay my dues. If I start serving time now, they'll take it off my sentence later. It'll bring me back to you sooner."

"Okay," she promised, her voice cracking.

There was no hiding the longing in his expression when he told her, "Thanks for helping me out of this jam."

"You were just arrested and you're *thanking* me?" she scoffed.

"If you truly believe you haven't done anything significant at this point, you're more delusional than I thought," he sniggered, shaking his head. "Once Redding gives up his buyer, I'll no longer have to worry if someone's after me. You have no idea what kind of stress I've been under."

Bexley shrugged. "Regardless, the *jam* you speak of isn't anywhere close to being pickled and jarred. Between the drugs planted in your storage unit, and uncovering what exactly went down in Mexico, I still have a lot of work ahead of me."

"You'll figure it out. Can you at least concede that we make a good team? We're close to bringing down a major drug dealer, Bex. In my book, getting narcotics off the streets is always a win."

"I wouldn't thank me just yet," she teased. "It's

going to take *a lot* of license plates to pay off your bill."

He lifted a lone eyebrow. "What if I make you one that's customized?"

She feigned a cheerleader-worthy squeal. "Ooo. Now we're talkin'! Could you bling it out with rhinestones around the edges?"

A chuckle died on his lips. "Promise me you'll be careful. Whoever's after me an' the guys probably knows you're involved. This isn't over until their boss is behind bars."

Deputy Peck appeared with another uniformed officer who scowled like he was having the worst day of his life. "Time's up," the other officer grunted.

"Try not to worry about me, Squires," Brewer said as the officers worked on opening the cell and untangling a set of leg chains. "Everything will work out." He flashed her a smirk that would affect anyone with a pulse. "I'll see you soon."

CHAPTER EIGHTEEN

Once she'd showered and changed into her pajamas, Bexley asked Red to forward the information she'd gathered regarding Brewer and the handful of young men who'd died of GSWs while Brewer was in Mexico. Bexley was convinced there'd been a hit on Brewer, and wanted to get on top of the situation in case law enforcement caught wind of his connection to a dead man.

As long as she kept herself occupied, she could honor her promise not to actively worry about Brewer's impending fate. Deciding the woman Brewer was kissing at Mikey's may be her best lead, it seemed another conversation with Colt Sawyer was in order. Fearing he'd washed his hands of her after their last encounter, she was pleasantly surprised when the MC president answered her call on the first ring.

"What can I do for you this time, darlin'?" he drawled.

"Brewer's been arrested for possession of cocaine," she told him.

"Sorry to hear it. But I'm still not—"

"No need to tiptoe around the subject. He disclosed his past involvement to me, including the reason he wanted to meet with you that night at Mikey's. I'm merely hoping to retrace his steps so we know how he ended up in Mexico. I believe the two incidents are directly related."

There was a long, weighted pause. Then he said, "In that case, I'll help in any way I can."

"Does Mikey have security cameras in his parking lot?"

"Sure does. Had them installed myself once we started usin' the bar as a meetin' place."

"I'm out-of-state at the moment, but I'll be heading back sometime tomorrow. Suppose you could get your hands on the footage from that night? I'm hoping to track this woman down through either a license plate or facial recognition."

"I'll see what I can do."

"Thanks, Colt. I'll be in touch."

As she ended the call, her laptop dinged with an email from Red.

"That girl is as efficient as she is eccentric," Bexley said aloud to the empty room.

By the time she'd thoroughly combed through the documents Red had attached, Bexley's gut rumbled demandingly. She checked her phone to confirm it was close to midnight, and she hadn't received any messages from Grayson.

The events of the day continually ran though her mind on an endless loop, some in excruciatingly slow detail. Whoever else had been at Redding's farm could be posted outside her motel room, waiting to catch her alone. Why didn't they rush the door? What were they waiting for? She debated looking out through the peephole, then the blinds, and finally stopped, positive food wasn't as important as staying alive until morning.

With that thought, sounds from the parking lot and adjoining rooms kept her alert for hours. She listened intently as a man argued with a woman over why he hadn't left his wife before Bexley heard the jingle of keys and a door closing in the room on her other side. There was no mistaking the deep rumble of Grayson's voice in the cough that followed.

It was some time after three in the morning when she finally passed out with her phone in one hand, and her stun gun tucked beside her thigh.

It felt as if she'd just closed her eyes when Bexley bolted awake to intense knocking on her motel door. Her phone buzzed a second later with a text from Grayson.

It's me. Let's go.

She stumbled from the bed, realizing she'd fallen asleep in jeans and a t-shirt. The dark room filled with daylight when she swung the door open. She squinted at Grayson. "You got in late. How'd it go?"

He breezed in past her. "Welder isn't talking. A sheriff's deputy said right after he was brought in, he made a call that spooked him. By the time I was allowed to pay him a visit in the hospital, he'd changed his mind about making a deal. I spent half the night trying to convince him otherwise."

Bexley's shoulders dropped. Redding's confession may've been the only way Brewer could walk away from the situation as a free man. But even that was a stretch. "What happens to Brewer now?"

"They're transporting him back to Papaya Springs later today," he said, taking an awkward stance in the middle of the room. He crossed and promptly uncrossed his arms while his gaze darted around the room. "Based on the information he gave Hawkins, the DA might be able to charge Welder with several felonies. It'd give me more leverage to convince him a deal's his best option." A deep-set scowl tugged at his features.

"What's wrong?" Bexley's eyes narrowed. "What aren't you telling me?"

"Nothing," he snapped, returning to the door. "We need to hit the road if we're going to catch our flight home."

After he closed the door behind him, Bexley spotted the lace on her satin pajama set peeking out from her luggage. It had been Grayson's gift to her on Valentine's Day.

BY THE TIME BEXLEY ARRIVED STRAIGHT FROM THE airport, Colt Sawyer was already waiting in her office, the fragrance of his leather club vest overpowering the coffee in her hand. "You're lookin' beat," he commented with a shrewd smirk. He leaned back in the chair and propped his black biker boots on the edge of her desk. "Somethin' keep you up all night, darlin'?"

Bexley nudged the door closed with her foot. "Maybe the thought of your wife coming after me because you insist on using outdated terms of endearment?" She eyed the biker sharply when he chuckled, then dropped her handbag on the credenza and plopped down into her chair. "Did you find the footage I asked for?"

He tossed a large white envelope across the desk. "One better. We tracked down her name, criminal record, and home address. My brothers rounded her up, and brought her into the clubhouse."

"You *kidnapped* her?"

"Not my style." Dimples pressed against his cheeks. "Gave 'er an incentive to come have a talk is all."

Bexley tried to imagine the girl's reaction when a gang of bikers showed up on her doorstep. Her head throbbed with an oncoming headache as she snatched the envelope and tore it open. Camila Gonzales had an extensive criminal history for only being twenty-five. She'd even done hard time for larceny and grand theft auto. Bexley glanced over the paper at Colt . "You're very resourceful."

"I have a little experience with this kind of thing…figured I'd save you some time. I'm just as eager to help Brewer. The guy deserves a break." He stood while running a hand through his wavy locks. "Come on, you can catch a ride with me."

Her phone dinged just then with a message from Luke.

Brewer is set to arrive in time for a 4:00 hearing

"I'll follow you," Bexley told Colt. "I have other errands to run."

The handsome biker stood and flashed a blindingly white-toothed grin. "Try to keep up."

———

On the clubhouse property, they passed a spacious garage where close to a dozen mechanics in club vests worked on hoisted motorcycles and classic cars. Although Bexley had paid a visit to the Inferno Glory MC home base once before, she decided by the light of day it didn't feel as sinister.

Maybe it had something to do with the fact that she was undercover last time, and had now become a comrade of sorts with Colt.

Inside the metal building, a group of Colt's brothers surrounded a young, olive-skinned woman sitting beneath a patriotic mural bearing the club's name. Between the woman's dark, sensual eyes; generous curves inside a small tank top and mini skirt; and lush black hair that spilled in large waves down to her waist, it didn't take a stretch of imagination to imagine Brewer's interest.

"Camila Gonzales?" Bexley asked, advancing closer. Tears streaked the woman's sharp cheek bones, highlighted with a shimmering bronzer. Bexley eyed Ranger, the giant who was always one step behind Colt. "Everything okay here?"

"I had no choice!" Camila blurted among a small sob. "They were going to send my brother to prison if I didn't hook up with that guy! I didn't know they were going to hurt him—I swear!" The woman bent over, shoulders trembling as she covered her face with both hands.

Bexley turned to Colt. "Can I have a minute alone with her?"

"Let's give them some space," Colt announced to his brothers. As the other men obediently shuffled outside, Colt gripped Bexley's elbow. "No offense, darlin', because I'm sure you can handle yourself, but I'm sticking around in case she tries to pull something. Never can be too careful."

With an appreciative nod, Bexley squatted down at the woman's side. "It's okay, Camila. They only brought you here because we're hoping you can help us piece together what happened to Brewer that night. Why don't you start from the beginning? Who contacted you about Brewer?"

Sniffling, Camila wiped her tears with her bare arm. "I don't know…some white guy…in a suit."

"Old? Young?" Bexley prodded. "Dark hair? No hair? Give me something to work with."

"He was like…my dad's age. Kind of skinny. Darkish hair." Camila scooted back in the chair and rolled her eyes like she was being inconvenienced. "I don't really remember anything else except he looked like the kind of average, middle class dude that you'd expect to knock on your door and try to sell you something."

Or someone with a government job,

Bexley perched on the couch beside the woman. "Where did he first approach you?"

"I was in the alley behind the hair salon, taking a

smoke break between clients. The dude just marched right up to me with a picture of Carlos on his phone, said my brother would spend the rest of his life behind bars if I didn't do everything exactly as he said."

"Had you seen the picture before? Did it look like something they'd taken off social media, or was it new—maybe something recent?"

"Lady, I have no idea." Camila shrugged her bare shoulders. "It was a picture of Carlos being Carlos. My brother's a thug."

Bexley arched an eyebrow. "Any chance Carlos dabbles in drug trafficking?"

"What are you, some kind of *cop*?" Camila snapped, darting to her feet. "I told you everything I know." Her eyes shifted to Colt. "Can I leave now?"

"I'm not a cop," Bexley assured her, standing. "I was hired to help the man you cat-fished. I'm trying to assess the reason he was kidnapped that night, and who organized it."

Camila's eyes rounded. "Wait, the hottie was *kidnapped?* You mean they didn't *kill* him?"

"Was that the plan?" Bexley asked. "Did they tell you he was going to die?" When Camila responded with a one-shouldered shrug, Bexley balled her hands into fists at her sides. "What happened after you left the bar with Brewer?"

"Things got hot and heavy real fast." The woman fanned herself with one hand. "I'm telling you, that man can kiss unlike anyone I've ever met. And his tongue—"

"I meant what happened *after* that," Bexley clarified, hoping neither of them noticed as her cheeks flushed hot. One way or another, she was about to lose her cool. "Why'd you think they killed him?"

"Because some scary dude came out of the dark and hit him over the head. The way the hottie dropped to the ground and started bleeding, I figured he had to be dead."

"What happened next?"

"They threw him into the passenger's side of a car, and told me I'd done a good job."

Bexley's stomach knotted. "And that was it? You didn't think to call for help, or ask where they were taking him?"

"Like I said, I thought he was dead."

"Did they warn you not to tell anyone?" Bexley pressed on. "Did they draw a weapon? Or did you simply not care?"

"They said my brother better be thankful I complied, then they left."

A little growl ripped through Bexley's throat. She'd had enough of this girl, and didn't know how to get through to her in a way that would be helpful. With as little information as she had provided, Bexley imagined a sketch artist wouldn't be able to create anything beyond stick figures.

Colt must've sensed her frustration the way he slid in at her side. "How many men were there?" he asked.

"Two," Camila answered. "One was really big, like a linebacker, and the other was pretty average looking."

Colt crossed his arms over his chest. "They both drove off with the unconscious man?"

"The big guy left in a black SUV, and the other one took off with the hottie."

"Did anything about the men stand out to you?" Bexley asked. "Do you remember any unusual features, or maybe something about the way they spoke? Was there anything about the vehicles that you can remember?"

Throwing an exaggerated shrug, Camila held her hands up by her head. "I mean it was dark, and I'd been drinking. Like, a lot. It's not like either of them were attractive or anything. What do you want from me?"

"A clear detail of *anything* would be nice," Bexley snarled. "You set a man up to be murdered, and you're handling the situation like a bad Tinder date!"

Camila stepped closer to Bexley. "If you have a problem with me, *chica*, maybe we should settle this outside!"

"Maybe we should!" Bexley shot back. "Maybe it'd knock some memories back into that gorgeous head!"

With a burst of laughter, Colt nudged his way between the women and pulled Bexley aside. "Okay, okay. I think that's enough questioning for now. Maybe *you* should step outside for a minute by yourself to cool down."

"Hold on!" Camila called out. "I just remembered something weird those guys said before they left!"

Bexley glanced around Colt, impatiently waiting for Camila to continue. She rolled her hand through the air. "Well?"

"The big dude…he told the little guy he'd meet him back at 'the Murder House' once he was done. The little guy laughed and said something like 'better not let the boss hear you call it that—he forbids anyone to mention Halliwell lived there'. Do you think they were talking about *Dean* Halliwell? Like that hot actor who went crazy and killed all those girls?"

Bits of the conversation Brewer and Bexley had with his friend Mugsy came flooding back to Bexley all at once.

"He's staying in one of those ridiculous mansions out past Highland Avenue," Mugsy had told them of Redding's last known whereabouts.

"It was owned by that actor," Brewer had added, "… the psycho that killed all those women."

Bexley's stomach plummeted.

They were using Dean Halliwell's house as their compound.

CHAPTER NINETEEN

O n the drive to Stronghold Investigations, Bexley called Red once again, this time requesting that she dig up the current deed holder on Dean Halliwell's property. Next she called Luke to check the status on Brewer's transfer, and was told even though he was a little ahead of schedule, they'd still see him at 4:00. Tension gripped her neck, wrenching her shoulders. She was running out of time to save Brewer, and she was terrified by the consequences of her failure.

J.J.'s new pickup truck was the only vehicle in their building's parking lot. He emerged from his office right as Bexley dashed inside. "Slow down," he drawled. "I was hopin' we could have us another talk."

"Where's Leona?" she asked, gesturing to the empty receptionist desk.

"In the hospital with pneumonia. Doc thinks she'll pull through, but either way I don't know that she'll be comin' back. She's not gettin' any younger. None of us are, I suppose." He scratched at his white hair. "You'll probably need to find yourself a new receptionist."

Bexley was beginning to worry there was a direct correlation to the old building and her coworkers' lungs. "You're entrusting *me* with the task?"

His white eyebrows shot up to his hairline. "You did agree to take over."

Bexley's heart plummeted. Amidst all the madness with Brewer's case, she'd completely forgotten about J.J.'s proposal to take over the business. "Oh…right."

"Before I forget, my attorney drew up some papers for you to sign—make the transfer of this place official." He stopped, hacking a little before he was able to continue. "You can take 'em home, have your attorney friend give 'em a look while you're at it, but I'm not tryin' to pull one over on you. It's pretty cut and dried. I paid this place off a decade ago, and now it's yours. I know it ain't much to look at, but you could always sell it and roll the profit into a new place. The business itself is always a struggle from month-to-month, but at the rate you're goin', you'll make more than enough to take care of yourself, and live a good life. Especially when I'm no longer on the payroll."

"Not so fast." Bexley's throat thickened. "What if I want to keep you on as a consultant?"

"It'd only be an occasional expense. I'm sure as hell not sitting in an office every damn day, waiting on you to call." His eyes lit and his cheeks spread with a wide grin. "I'm planning on buying me a fishin' boat—spending my retirement the proper way. I'm on my way to look at one now. Cross your fingers it's as good in person as it looks on paper."

"This is all happening kinda fast." Bexley wrapped her arms around her waist, hoping his plans meant his diagnosis wasn't as grim as she feared. "Are you sure you want to entrust your life's work to a rookie?"

"There's no one else I'd rather see take over." J.J. patted her shoulder. "Life tends to happen fast to the best of us, sweetheart. All a person can do is hold on and enjoy the ride while you can. Speaking of riding, how did things go in Iowa with your friend?"

"Not as planned. He was arrested—turned himself in, actually. And we brought down a shooter who seriously injured Brewer's friend." Her eyes shifted past J.J. when a wealth of emotions clogged her throat. "Someone wants Brewer dead, and I'm terrified I won't be able to save him."

J.J. eyed her with a tilt of his head. "Sounds like you're personally invested in this case."

Lying to her mentor had never been easy. "Brewer has become important to me," she admitted with a guilt-ridden look. "He seems convinced I can get him out of this mess, but I'm worried I'm too close to him to properly do my job."

Glancing thoughtfully across the room, J.J. scratched at his chin. "Want my advice?"

Bexley rolled her eyes. "You may as well ask if I want Pollo's tacos."

J.J. turned to her, brows furrowed with confusion. "Come again?"

"The answer will always be yes," she explained, winking.

"You're far more capable than you realize. It's time you come to terms with that. If he believes in you, maybe you need to believe in yourself too. You have what it takes to help this Brewer person. As for your relationship with 'im, if it's meant to happen, it'll fall into place on its own over time. No need to rush things."

As she absorbed his advice, she blinked back at him with a blank expression. It was almost the exact opposite of what he'd once told her in regards to her relationship with Grayson. Back then, he'd said life was short, and encouraged her to go for it without hesitation.

Did he sense things were different with Brewer, or was he being cautious for other reasons? Did he sense *she* was somehow different? She certainly didn't feel the same kind of pressure she'd felt with Grayson.

J.J. pulled a worn baseball cap from his back pocket, and slipped it over his white hair. "Papers are in a manila envelope on my desk with your name typed on the outside. Holler if you have any questions."

Watching him stroll out of the office toward the parking lot, her stomach began to twist. Was she really ready to run the place on her own? It didn't seem she had any other choice. She wouldn't dream of asking him to change his plans. He deserved to spend the time he had left however he wanted.

She retrieved the thick envelope from his office,

taking a moment to inhale the rich scent of tobacco that lingered from all the years J.J. had sat at his desk, puffing on a pipe while attempting to solve one of a thousand cases. She'd miss his constant encouragement and words of wisdom as much as she'd miss seeing his sideways smirk every morning.

Feeling a little despondent, she sat at her own desk to check her emails. A handful of minutes passed before Red's name flashed across her smart phone's screen.

"What'd you find?"

"Dean Halliwell's property was purchased three weeks ago with cold, hard cash by a bogus corporation," Red reported in a rush. "Someone tried to bury their tracks, but they didn't do a very thorough job. It only took me a few minutes to track down the social security number linked to the corporation. Seems it was created by Papaya Springs's own Mayor Edward Hoffman."

Bexley slapped her desk. "I *knew* it!"

"Hold onto your undies, because I have some more ground-breaking news. I uncovered some more deets on one of the young men who died near Tijuana last weekend. It seems Martín López—*real name* Victor Martínez—is tied to the Mexican cartel, and his death has created some major conflict over the border. Probably because his father is *the head* of the cartel, one Mr. Francisco Martínez. Victor was given an alias at a young age in an attempt to keep him off the hit list of Francisco's enemies, but his identity wasn't wiped clean enough to escape my radar. Daddy dearest escaped from a California prison less than a year ago after serving two out of twenty years on a felony drug conviction. Wanna guess where Francisco's originating arrest took place?"

"Victor's father has close ties to Papaya Springs," Bexley surmised, digging through her folders until she found the information she already had on Victor. "Good to know."

"The cartel put a hefty reward out for anyone who can produce Victor's assassin."

Alarm rattled Bexley's bones. If Brewer had killed Victor, even if in self-defense, he'd have even bigger problems than those already on his plate.

"Red, you're killing this job." Bexley drummed her fingertips against the manila envelope containing J.J.'s gift. "Listen…I know it's lightyears beneath your skill set, but would you happen to be interested in working for me as an occasional receptionist in addition to being my technical expert? I'm taking over the business soon, and can't promise you a pay grade anything close to what you'd make for the FBI, but I need someone to keep me in line…prevent this place from going under."

"I'm in. Anyone who throws a *Star Wars* reference into casual conversation is alright with me. Besides, being your Padawan is a *thousand* times more engaging than IT work."

"Being my what?" With a harsh laugh, Bexley shook her head. "You know what, forget it. I'm excited to officially bring you on board, Red. You certainly bring…*life* to this place. And you're one smart…ah…Wookiee?"

"You're already speaking my language. It's like we were destined to work together."

"Plan on coming in Monday morning. I'll give you a run down of the basics you need to know about this place, and we'll talk more about your duties. Then we can talk about updating the computer system to something from the current decade."

"You will not regret one nanosecond of this decision!"

Ending the call with another shake of her head, Bexley grabbed her handbag. On the way to the parking lot, she called Kiersten. "I have a huge favor to ask."

"Are you kidding?" Kiersten's bright voice sang. "I'm indebted to you for life after what you did! You could ask for my first born and I'd hand him on over!"

"Why is it a 'him'? Oh my god, are you trying to tell me something?"

"Of course not. Luke and I aren't there...*yet*."

Bexley sighed. She wasn't ready for her inner circle to include dirty diapers and drooling hair-pullers. "Do you think you could get down to the courthouse for a four o'clock hearing? They're expecting Brewer to appear on felony charges. Luke's his attorney—he can fill you in on the details. If he's released, I want you to give him the spare key to my apartment. He'll need a place to stay."

"Where will you be?" Kiersten demanded.

"I have to look into something related to his case."

Kiersten clicked her tongue. "Who would've thought one day Sexy Bexley would be lusting after the kid voted most likely to become the next unabomber?"

"First of all, there's no lusting on my part, and secondly, be nice. Our classmates probably say the same thing about you and me. Besides, there's more to Brewer than you know."

"No one's *blaming* you. I'm simply pointing out that the man has changed. Like completely." She took a hesitant breath. "Does Grayson know about your budding romance?"

Bexley closed her eyes. She wasn't going to lie to her best friend either. "He has his suspicions. I keep telling him there's nothing there, but I think I was wrong. I need to let Grayson know it's over between us so we can both move on. Only I don't know how to do it without hurting him. He's a good man— just not the right one for me."

"Let me give it a try. We both know he's incredibly stubborn when it comes to your relationship. Maybe he needs to hear it from someone else."

"Thanks, Kiersten. You're a good friend." Heaving a sigh, Bexley climbed into her SUV. "Listen, I need to get going. I'll catch up with you later tonight."

"Whatever you're up to, please be careful. I have a feeling I'm going to need a maid of honor soon, and there's no one else who could possibly fill that position."

Despite the warm rays that came with the afternoon sunlight, the sight of Dean Halliwell's elaborate mansion alongside the roaring ocean sent several cold, mind-numbing chills down Bexley's spine. After she'd been drugged and attacked by the Hollywood actor inside one of the guest rooms, she never would've dreamed of returning for any reason. Yet there she sat in her vehicle across the street, watching as two guards carried on a conversation inside the gated property.

Although she'd gone there intending only to case the joint and observe any activity, her curiosity was too strong to resist. Whoever was the mastermind behind the drugs and the fate of Brewer's crew could be inside, thinking they were untouchable. It wasn't in her skill set to simply sit back and let them get by with ruining the life of someone she cared about.

She snagged her handbag off the passenger's seat, digging around inside it for her stun gun. When her fingertips brushed over the cool metal of her pistol, she sucked in a deep breath. She'd swung by her place to grab it after leaving the office, deciding if she were to confront the heavy-hitting criminals on her own, she wasn't about to do it unarmed. Plus she was certain she'd seen the bulge of weapons beneath the guards' jackets. And after all the time she'd spent at shooting ranges with Grayson and Cineste, it wasn't like she was inept with the weapon.

Against her strongest desire to leave the gun behind, she tucked it into the back of her jeans before slipping from the vehicle. The guards were deep enough into their conversation that they didn't seem to notice as she darted across the street. Having been to the mansion several times before, even once spending the night as Dean Halliwell's guest, she had the advantage of knowing the property's layout. If luck was on her side, they hadn't bothered to update the location of Halliwell's security cameras. She crept along the thick bushes meant to block the prying eyes of Halliwell's fans, and headed toward the ocean where she'd have an unobscured view.

Very little had changed since the night she helped Grayson bring Halliwell down for multiple murders. The landscaping was a bit overgrown and the cushions were missing from the dozens of patio furniture pieces filling the backyard patio, otherwise it was as if the actor could still be taking residence there. Bexley shuddered with the thought.

Luckily, the secret fence built into the shrubbery

was still in place, and hadn't been locked. She carefully pushed it open, remembering it tended to rust from lack of use.

As she crept closer toward the mansion, her ears perked with the sound of a deep voice rumbling with anger from the open patio doors. "…if someone witnessed you entering the property? We can't be seen together!"

"I came here because I need to know why that biker still isn't dead!"

Bexley sucked in a sharp breath. She *knew* the baritone voice that answered.

"Silencing him has been difficult from the very start," the deeper voice volleyed.

She knew that voice too. She grabbed her phone and quickly activated the voice recording app before inching closer.

"They shouldn't have sent an amateur punk to do the job!" the deeper voice continued.

"That *amateur punk* was the son of Francisco Martínez, you fool! I wasn't about to turn down an offer from the cartel! Do you think he would've volunteered to send his son had he known the boy's identity had been compromised? Since Martínez escaped prison, the hit list on his family has grown to the size of the Baja peninsula!"

It didn't sound as if Brewer had killed Victor Martínez. At the same time she felt a surge of relief, an angry tremor slipped through her. Whoever was speaking was responsible for kidnapping Brewer and clearly wanted him dead.

The deeper voice grunted. "If you'd been more careful with Hawkins's child and fiancée all those years ago, we'd still have significant leverage over him!"

"I had to get his attention," the baritone voice replied. "She wasn't supposed to die. Killing women and children isn't my thing."

"Well you'll have to come up with a foolproof plan. Hawkins is smarter than the other Coasties involved. He brought down my team in Iowa before we had a chance to take Welder out. And now that he got that nosy investigator involved—"

"Do not stand there and tell me you're backing down because of a gun-toting Barbie!"

That's something I haven't been called before, Bexley thought to herself. *Barbie as in oddly flexible with great hair?*

"She's more clever than you think," the deeper voice answered.

"Nonsense! Bexley Squires is completely harmless *and* incompetent! You wouldn't be standing here as a free man if that weren't true!"

"Rude," Bexley breathed.

"It's your fault for not taking her and that detective of yours out months ago," the deeper voice grumbled. "If he still can't be persuaded to switch sides after all these years, then it's time to get rid of him!"

A lump rose in Bexley's throat. *That detective of yours.*

"Rivers is too good at his job!" the baritone voice snapped. "If I don't have a valid reason to fire him, it'll raise all kinds of red flags! We can't afford that kind of attention!"

"So *create* a valid reason! Either that, or stage an accident! Rig his car! Hire a convict to shoot him! I don't care how you do it—just make him *and Squires* disappear! I don't understand why she isn't gone by now either! We aren't going to get to Hawkins and his remaining crew until she's out of the picture, and we can't afford to be linked to the drugs! If the cartel doesn't make good on their threats to clean up the mess we've made—*including* the two of us— we'll both end up in prison for the rest of our lives!"

That's the money shot, Bexley thought.

Anger clenched her chest as she stormed toward

the back door. She first spotted the tall, gaunt mayor lingering behind the same elaborate bar where Dean Halliwell once served her champaign. It didn't faze Bexley in the slightest to see him with her own eyes since she'd recently learned he'd purchased the property, and she'd suspected his involvement since the beginning.

What shook her to the core was the overweight man standing on the other side of the bar, across from the mayor.

The one with the baritone voice.

Grayson's boss.

CHAPTER TWENTY

"Lieutenant Baker?" Bexley blurted.

When his eyes met hers, the lieutenant's jaw clenched and his gaze narrowed.

Mayor Hoffman snarled, "How in the hell did you get in here?"

"The gig is up, gentlemen." Bexley squared her shoulders and stood taller, drawing courage from the fact that J.J. and Brewer believed in her. "This *gun-toting Barbie* caught you red handed this time."

Lieutenant Baker held the palms of his hands upright in a peaceful gesture. "I don't know what you *think* you heard—"

"Grayson always suspected you were being influenced by someone outside of the force," Bexley interrupted with a shake of her head, "but I don't ever think he ever imagined you'd be in charge of something so diabolical and corrupt."

"And what exactly is it you think I've done?" the lieutenant challenged, raising an eyebrow.

"Drug trafficking, federal embezzlement, murder, kidnapping, *attempted* murder…and that's only the start. I'm not an attorney, so you'll have to give me a minute to make the complete list."

In the next heartbeat, the metallic click of a pistol cocking rang in Bexley's ear.

Her skin erupted with goosebumps with the sound of DA Jenkins' voice. "That won't be necessary. You're trespassing on private property. Pursuant to California law, I'm allowed to use deadly force to protect myself from bodily harm."

Bexley's heart plummeted.

It was foolish to think she could easily bring their crimes to justice after they'd been successfully running drugs for so many years.

This time, she'd underestimated the situation.

She'd made a fatal mistake.

The mayor smiled at Jenkins over her shoulder. "The timing couldn't be better. We can finally get rid of her once and for all."

"On your knees, Squires," Jenkins hissed.

Bexley remained standing. "Okay, but you fellas might want to think this through a little more," she warned, willing her body to stop trembling. "My boss is well aware that I was coming to this property, and the mayor's social security number is tied to the deed. Don't you think that will raise some unsavory questions?"

"Is that true?" Baker hissed, turning to his partner.

Mayor Hoffman blanched at the other two men. "I didn't…I mean…"

"You blubbering idiot!" Jenkins yelled behind her. "Do you realize what you've done?"

"Do it," Baker urged, dipping his chin. "Take her out. If she walks away from this, we won't be able to fix it. I'll fashion a plausible explanation."

A long, slow breath fell from Bexley's lips.

The faint sound of the trigger being pulled amplified a thousand times.

She jerked her head back, striking her skull against Jenkins' face.

Jenkins cried out and fell against something, sending it clattering to the floor.

At the same time, a bullet whizzed over her head.

Lieutenant Baker yelped in pain.

The gun fell to the floor at Bexley's feet.

The mayor charged forward, diving for the gun.

She got to it first.

The mayor grabbed a fistful of her hair.

Despite the blinding pain, Bexley fought against the older man with everything she had. Within seconds, she overpowered his weak grip, and gained complete control of the pistol. The mayor froze with his hands up in the air. "You don't have the courage to pull the trigger," he challenged.

She released the safety. "Sure you wanna take the chance?" She backed away from him, including Jenkins in her range. "Go stand by your buddy. Both of you get down on the floor, hands where I can see them."

She searched for the lieutenant over her shoulder, but he was nowhere to be seen. He had, however, left behind a small spot of blood. *The bullet must've nicked him.*

She turned back to her captor. "Hey, Siri!" she shouted. "Call Emergency Services!"

"Calling Emergency Services in five seconds," the robotic voice replied from inside her jeans pocket.

"It really works!" Bexley said, beaming at the two men. "I didn't think it would really work!"

"Siri, cancel!" Hoffman yelled. "Cancel!"

"Cancel call!" Jenkins tried. "No, Siri!"

Bexley clicked her tongue against the roof of her mouth. "Maybe you should try scratching her belly and giving her a treat."

A loud commotion came from the other room. Bexley already guessed she was in trouble before she saw the two armed guards running at her.

"Drop the weapon!" one roared, threatening her with an assault rifle. The other guard stood behind him, appearing confused by the situation.

Bexley held her ground. "I'd rather you drop yours."

"Calling Emergency Services," Siri reported before a ring tone came from her pocket.

"Shit!" the 50-something guard yelled. "Siri, cancel! Cancel, Siri! Don't call them!"

"It won't work," the mayor told him. "I already tried."

"Your generation has a lot to learn about smart phones," Bexley scolded, rolling her eyes.

"Nine-one-one, what's your emergency?" a woman's voice asked.

"This is private investigator Bexley Squires. Tell Detective Grayson Rivers that I'm being held at gun point by Mayor Hoffman, DA Jenkins, and

Lieutenant Baker's thugs at Dean Halliwell's former residence. No need for the address, Rivers will know exactly where to find us. You may want to send several squad cars and an ambulance, too."

The guards exchanged a knowing look before they fled from the room.

Bexley tipped her head in their direction while flashing a smirk between the mayor and DA. "Should've given them more drug money."

"You still don't have any evidence to support your theory," the mayor snarled in a quiet voice.

"I'm sure they can find something in this house that will prove your guilt. Don't you know it's bad luck to take refuge in a serial killer's home? I mean, Dean Halliwell was arrested just a few rooms down."

"Officers are on their way, Miss Squires," the dispatcher called out. "They should be there in less than five minutes. Are you in immediate danger?"

"I secured the weapon," Bexley replied. "I'm holding the mayor and DA until help arrives, but you need to let them know that Lieutenant Baker got away. And I'm pretty sure he was shot by one of his partners."

The mayor bared his teeth like a feral animal. "What will it take for you to realize that I'm untouchable? How many times do we have to play this game?"

Bexley's gaze narrowed. "Hate to break it to you, *Mayor*, but you're being recorded by nine-one-one. The only game you'll be playing from this point forward will be 'don't drop the soap'."

GRAYSON WAS THE FIRST TO ENTER THE ROOM IN A tactical vest, weapon drawn. His terse expression disappeared the second he assessed the situation, and realized Bexley was unharmed. He lowered his arms. "Are you okay?"

She nodded, also lowering her aching arms before engaging the safety. She watched as several uniformed officers entered the room, cuffing the mayor and DA's hands behind their backs.

Bexley turned to Grayson, pointing the muzzle downward as she handed the weapon over. Grayson took a handkerchief from his pocket before taking the pistol. "Whose is this?"

"Jenkins had it. He accidentally shot your lieutenant instead of me."

"He shot at you?" he growled, eyeing Jenkins with a flash of dark malice.

"Never mind that. Did you get my message about Lieutenant Baker?"

"I don't understand what happened here. Why'd you think he's involved?"

"Because I overheard him talking with the mayor about their failed attempts to kill Brewer Hawkins. And Otis Welder. *And* you and me. They mentioned the cartel and drugs, too. I believe they're responsible for funneling cocaine seized by the Coast Guard to the cartel in Mexico."

"Nonsense!" the mayor objected. "You have no basis for these claims!"

"I can replay the conversation for you if you'd like," Bexley told him. "I have it recorded on my phone."

"Keep your mouth *shut*, Hoffman," Jenkins warned. "Not another word until you've talked with your attorney."

"Guess that won't be you this time," Bexley prodded with a wink.

Grayson wiped a hand over his face, and then gripped the back of his neck. For a moment, he seemed to doubt Bexley's accusation—she knew by the simple look he was giving her. She'd seen it a hundred times. It was all the confirmation she needed to know she could never go back to him.

He finally stopped one of the uniformed officers as the others escorted a tight-lipped mayor from the room. "Send two squad cars over to Lieutenant Baker's home. *Immediately*. Let them know he could be armed and dangerous."

"Yessir," the officer answered.

Grayson started after him. Bexley snagged his coat sleeve, reeling him back to her. "Where are you going?"

"To the lieutenant's house." His brow furrowed. "If you're right and he *is* involved, maybe I can talk some sense into him before someone gets hurt."

"I know you're shocked to hear your superior isn't the man you thought he was, but trust me, *I am* right about this. And I want to be there when you take the crooked bastard down."

THE LIGHT OF A HELICOPTER BLINKED OVER THEIR heads in the dark sky as Bexley and Grayson stood behind a squad car in matching tactical vests. The SWAT team was stationed around the lieutenant's home from all sides, and a sniper held position from the rooftop of a nearby hardware store. They'd been camped out in the same positions for several hours as Lieutenant Baker threatened to shoot anyone who approached the two-story cottage. His wife and daughter were believed to be inside with him.

"Do you believe me yet?" Bexley snapped at Grayson.

"Maybe next time you'll think twice about investigating something of this caliber on your own," he snapped back. "You should've called me."

Bexley's patience for the entire situation was wearing thin. She'd been texting back and forth with both Kiersten and Brewer since his hearing, and was relieved to hear he'd been released on bail pending a trial. She was eager to head home.

Grayson stood taller with the sight of Deputy Danks and the SWAT team commander approaching. "He's accepting our request to release his family," the fit, gray-haired commander reported. "His wife and daughter are on their way out."

A second later, Bexley's stomach dropped as she watched Tammy and Violet scurry from the house. Their faces were both streaked with mascara, and they had a wild look in their eyes that Bexley doubted she'd ever forget.

The women had safely crossed the yellow caution tape when there was a distant *bang* that made everyone in the vicinity flinch. It sounded as if it was coming from the commander's two-way radio.

"Shots fired! Shots fired!"

The SWAT team members closed in on the house with the precision and ease of a ballet class. Bexley held her breath as they stormed through the front door. She was sure everyone held their breath until they heard the commander's two-way radio crackle. *"Target shot himself. Lieutenant Baker is dead."*

The lieutenant's wife cried out, sinking to her knees. Suddenly, their daughter was charging at Bexley. "This is your fault!" Violet screamed among a sob. "You made my father do this! If it wasn't for you, he'd still be alive!"

Before Bexley had a chance to step back, Violet swung a fist and caught Bexley above her eye. Deputy Danks rushed in to take the distraught teenager away. By the time he'd pushed Violet into the back of the nearest squad car, Bexley was shaking. She'd done the right thing, she'd found the killers and brought them to justice. Brewer was safe. And everything was going to be alright. So why didn't she feel good about it?

Grayson turned without another word and left her, still bleeding from Violet's attack.

"I did the right thing!" Bexley shouted at his back. She wiped at the blood over her eye and turned to glare at the car where Violet was still pounding on the window and screaming at her. "I did the right thing," she repeated to herself.

CHAPTER TWENTY-ONE

Outside the Mediterranean steakhouse, Bexley's dark hair fluttered across her face in the brisk ocean air while her stomach twisted with unease. She hadn't invited Grayson to their family dinners when they were together, and she knew her father's reaction to the presence of a man on bail who wanted to be a regular part of Bexley's life would be extreme. Especially when her father had arranged the dinner solely because he claimed to have "something important" to tell the sisters. Bexley shuddered when considering the possibilities.

When she pulled her hair aside and turned to her date for the night, her heart thumped in heavy staccatos. A short stubble lined Brewer's jaw, and he'd grown his hair out on the sides to match the shorter length on top. In a plain black t-shirt under his black leather jacket and black jeans, he could almost be mistaken for a hipster were it not for his extensive tattoo collection and the overall vibe of mystique that seeped from his pores. He flashed one of his sexy smirks, warm chestnut eyes sparkling in the moonlight.

It wasn't only his exceptionally good looks that drew her to Brewer. After all the mayhem they'd survived together, a mutual attachment had formed between them. They'd wordlessly shifted into a more involved relationship that had yet to go beyond a lot of hand-holding and flirting, but the magnetism between them crackled more than ever. She spent a lot of sleepless nights thinking about him as he slept in her apartment's spare room. Things were moving quickly, and she wasn't sure she was ready.

"This evening will probably feel a lot like you're getting all your teeth pulled at once by a shoddy dentist in a dark alley," she blurted, twisting her arms in front of her. "But my sister's boyfriend will be here, and I think you two will get along. Alex is a decent guy. The two of you can suffer through the torment of my old man together."

With a deliciously dark chuckle, Brewer pulled

her in close, tucking her against his side. "You forget I was in the military. I can handle his type without breaking a sweat." He pressed a kiss to the top of her head that shot ripples of warmth down to her toes.

Slipping her arm around his waist, she let out a hefty sigh and wondered if it was too late to back out of the dinner. She could list several activities she'd rather be doing with Brewer that would be far more enjoyable. "I still don't think you're prepared for Captain Ferguson."

He leaned away from her. "Worried what he'll think of me?"

"Of course not!" she scolded. When he cocked an eyebrow in question, she huffed. "It's not what you think."

"I get it, Squires. The tattoos, my pending trial…I'm not the kind of guy a girl dreams about bringing home to meet her dad."

"You don't understand. My father's opinion doesn't matter." She gripped his chin in her hand. "No one's opinion of you matters to me, Brewer Hawkins. What I once said about you being a bad boy…I didn't mean it. Not the way you think. While it seems you have an affinity for living on the wild side, *I* know you're a good man. No one could ever change my mind."

Brewer's pupils dilated as he bent down to brush his soft lips over hers. Though it was a sweet, harmless kiss that felt more like a thank you, Bexley's insides exploded like fireworks and her mind became numb. She closed her eyes for a moment, drawing her lips into her mouth as she savored his sweet taste.

He drew back. "You have no idea how long I've wanted to do that."

Lungs seizing with a sharp breath, her eyelids flipped open. She hooked her arm around his neck and brought his lips back down to meet hers. The kiss was far more intense, heightened by months of longing and uncertainty. Bexley melted against the warmth of his body, allowing his strong arms to hold her upright. His lips were as strong as the fist anchored in her hair, as if he was determined to finally show her his true feelings.

I must be certifiable for not doing this sooner, Bexley found herself thinking. The sensations that overwhelmed her from head to toe were too divine for her to ever want it to stop.

With the sound of a fake cough, however, they quickly jumped apart.

"Whoa!" Cineste exclaimed, openly gaping. Snuggled against Alex's side, she wore a pink floral dress that fit her like a glove, and her hair fell over her shoulders in perfectly curled soft waves. For a moment, Bexley wondered if the sight of her beautiful sister made Brewer regret choosing to be with someone who considered vanity to be a luxury.

Cineste's eyes remained wide. "Bex! Who the hell's the hottie?"

Bexley's hands trembled a little as they smoothed over her hair. "He's Hawk—I mean he's not a *hawk*-hawk, his name is Hawk—I mean *Hawkins*." Warmth rushed through her cheeks as she blinked helplessly back at her sister.

Chuckling, Brewer extended his hand. "You can call me Brewer."

"Cineste," she answered, still looking baffled when she took his hand. "This is Alex."

As the two men shook hands among shared smiles, Bexley threw her sister a guilty look. "I've been meaning to tell you that Grayson and I went our separate ways. There just never seemed to be a good time to bring it up in conversation."

"I've known for awhile," Cineste said with a casual shrug. "I decided something was up and figured you wouldn't tell me, so I asked Kiersten."

The heaviness of guilt festering in Bexley's chest all at once lifted with her sister's acceptance. "Maybe if we hurry inside, we can do a round of shots before the captain arrives." She gave Brewer a lopsided smile. "You'll thank me later."

"She's right," Alex agreed, holding open the heavy door to the establishment. "You'll need it."

Bexley and her sister passed through the doorway as the two men chatted with ease behind them. The loud clamor of conversation and forks clinking against plates in the bright, clean atmosphere of the restaurant instantly drowned out the details of their conversation.

After Bexley checked in with the hostess, letting her know they'd be at the bar while waiting for their father, Cineste gripped her elbow. "This is the old classmate who was busted for selling cocaine?"

"Just how much did Kiersten tell you?" Bexley grumbled. She wasn't accustomed to her personal affairs being passed around her inner circle.

"Not nearly enough. Your busy schedule needs to allot for more sister time."

They claimed side-by-side stools at the modern slab of walnut that stretched across the bar, and their men stood right behind them. Bexley was instantly flustered when Brewer's fingertips settled on her waist. "I'm guessing a shot of whiskey is out of the question," he teased, brushing his lips over her earlobe as he spoke.

Her body ignited. "Tequila!" she choked out, motioning to the male bartender. "We're gonna need four double-shots of tequila!"

Cineste giggled at her side. "You don't mess around, sis."

"I thought *I* was the one who liked living on the wild side," Brewer teased.

The bartender poured the shots in front of them before handing out lime wedges and a salt shaker. Bexley threw two twenties on the table, and handed the glasses out to everyone.

"Here's to new adventures," Brewer declared, holding his glass over Bexley's shoulder. The foursome clinked their lowball glasses together and then licked the salt from their hands before slugging the strong liquid back and sucking on the limes.

"Woo!" Bexley shouted, setting her glass down. "If that won't prepare you for an evening with our old man, nothing will!"

"Am I *that* intolerable?" their father called out behind them.

Bexley froze in place.

"Dad!" Cineste spun around and jumped off

her stool. "Bex is just nervous about you meeting her new boyfriend."

Bexley was ready to strangle her sister by the time she turned to them. But she stopped short and her stomach hardened with the sight of a pretty blonde at their father's side. The petite woman wore a short, bright red dress with a plunging neckline. Both the dress and the woman's beige heels showed evidence of being well-worn—possibly from a second-hand store. Her honeyed locks hung limp down to her chin in a cheap bob, and her makeup was heavily applied in a cartoonish manner. She couldn't have been a day older than Bexley.

A sudden burst of anger shot through Bexley. She suspected the woman was directly related to his announcement of "something important," and she wasn't having it. Their father was determined to destroy what was left of their family.

"Wife number four, so soon?" she quipped. "And they say millennials and boomers don't get along."

The captain's face darkened to the shade of a beet. "Bite your tongue, young lady," he snarled, wrapping his arm around the woman's shoulders. "Sadie is *not* my wife."

Bexley clicked her tongue. "In that case, I hope

he paid you for the night upfront, *Sadie*," she told the woman, "You're gonna want to split once you get to know *the real* Captain Ferguson."

Behind her, Brewer gripped her arm. "Bex," he warned under his breath.

"That is enough!" Bexley's father roared. *"Sadie is your sister!"*

A hush fell over the bar patrons as they shot curious gazes at the dysfunctional family.

Cineste slapped her hands over her mouth.

Bexley staggered backwards, colliding with Brewer. She was vaguely aware of his arms encircling her, providing a superficial surge of comfort.

Bexley and Cineste had another sister. Did their mother know?

Bexley's eyes flickered between the woman and their father. "How old?" she heard herself ask.

The captain's angry expression evened out. "She was born five months after you."

Vomit burned Bexley's throat.

He had an affair, and started another family.

"I'm not proud of what I did to your mother," he continued, "but I don't regret bringing Sadie into the world. I've kept this secret from you girls for too long. You deserve to have your sister in your lives."

"You *bastard!*" Cineste cried. "Mom raised us by herself all those years while you were deployed on the other side, and you weren't there for her when she got sick! She deserved so much better!"

Alex stepped in beside her, taking her by the shoulders and whispering something in her ear.

Vision blurred, Bexley stumbled past her father and the woman. *Her sister.* It was too much. She needed fresh air before she suffocated on her father's revelation.

The racket of her father and Cineste arguing faded away as she passed the hostess and continued outside. She crossed the deserted road and kicked her shoes off in the sand. A beat later, she sensed Brewer coming up behind her.

"Do you want me to take you home?" he asked.

"I can't deal with this," Bexley told him, spinning around to face him. Her breaths fell in hot, tight huffs across her lips. "I can't deal with him. I can't deal with *her.*"

"You don't have to deal with them if you don't want to." With an understanding look, he squeezed her shoulders. "Just breathe."

She inhaled a deep breath, savoring the saltiness of the air. Her shoulders hunched forward on an exhale. The beach was her favorite place, and the sound of the crashing waves behind them already did wonders to calm her fury.

Brewer slipped a hand inside hers, and gently tugged. "Let's take a walk."

After several minutes of walking silently hand-in-hand, the drama from the restaurant began to fade. She stopped Brewer alongside the shore, standing on her toes for another kiss. It was shorter and not as passionate as their last, but it eased her nerves.

"Thank you," she said, resting her forehead against his chin when they were finished.

His thick fingers kneaded the back of her neck. "Do you want to talk about it?"

"Not really."

He guided her back several yards, pulling her down to sit at his side in the dry sand. He retrieved a lighter and pack of smokes from inside his jacket. "Isabella cheated on me once," he told her while lighting a cigarette. "Overheard her on the phone telling him not to call anymore because it was over. Thought it was the worst feeling I'd ever had, knowing she'd been with another man. Happened a few months before she found out she was pregnant." Smoke streamed from his nostrils as he stared at the horizon. "Felt guilty for wondering if the baby was really mine, but couldn't help it. I think any man in my situation would've had the same fear."

Bexley sensed unfathomable pain in his confession, and wondered if he'd ever recover from the loss of his unborn child, even if he were to one day start a new family. Stomach clenching, she turned to him. "There's something I have to tell you." She stopped to lick her lips, choosing her next words with care. "Grayson stopped by my office today."

Brewer's eyes returned to the horizon. "Oh yeah?" He flicked the ash of his cigarette while grinding his jaw. "Did you send your ex my regards?"

Though she was slightly flattered by the tinge of jealousy in his tone, her muscles became rigid as she recalled the painful reunion before she clocked out for the day. As promised, Kiersten had told Grayson of Bexley's budding relationship with Brewer, and gently suggested it was time to let Bexley go. Grayson had merely tossed an envelope on the desk, and didn't even make eye contact. Then he was gone again. Any hope of saving their decade-old friendship had fizzled with the cold visit.

"He gave me a copy of a ten-page confession written by Lieutenant Baker," Bexley explained.

"They discovered it while searching his house after he died. I read it, and came across something significant…something you deserve to know." She took one of Brewer's hands and gave a gentle squeeze. "It had to do with Isabella."

His nostrils flared, and his entire body vibrated. "That cold son-of-a-bitch looked me in the eye, told me someone had attacked my fiancée and killed my son. He's the one who killed her, isn't he?"

Slowly nodding, she entwined their fingers. "He didn't do it intentionally—at least not right away. He'd gone to your place that morning, right after you left, and flashed his badge to get inside. He threatened to have her parents deported if she didn't convince you to become his mule. She refused to comply…said she'd turn him into the cops if he went after you or her family. That's when he decided to hurt her." She swallowed the lump rising in her throat. "He figured if he hurt her enough, you'd have no other choice than to take Redding up on his offer."

Brewer snapped his hand out from hers and silently inhaled the cigarette, eyes unblinking as he stared straight ahead, shoulders taut. Bexley felt as if she had witnessed him break, and it stabbed her right through the heart.

She was suddenly embarrassed by her reaction to meeting Sadie. In light of what Brewer had gone through, discovering the captain had an affair, and produced another child didn't seem quite as dire.

"I know it's a lot to absorb," she told him in a shaking voice. "I'm so sorry they hurt you like that, Brewer. You didn't deserve it. Neither did Isabella. Nor your baby." There wasn't anything more she could say, and there certainly wasn't anything she could do to make things right for him. She moved to stand. "I'll give you time to process this alone."

"No." His warm fingers clamped around her wrist, and his eyes moved away from the dark water to meet her gaze. She couldn't decide if he was crying, or she merely saw a reflection of light flash in his dark eyes. Either way, she sensed he needed her comfort. "I want you here."

With a nod, she settled in beside him, leaning her head against his shoulder.

As they silently watched the waves roll in, Bexley admitted to herself that her life in general could be so much worse. Despite being shot at several times and questioning her sleuthing skills, she'd inherited a successful business, and brought down a couple of bad guys disguised as community leaders. Her family situation had always been a bit rocky, but she'd grown close to Cineste and Alex. Maybe she could find a way to let this new half-sister into her life too. She'd accumulated a handful of friends she could count on to have her back—Red included—and now a kind man with a big heart wanted her to stick around.

She slipped her hand into the crook of Brewer's arm. There was only one way to go and that was forward. She couldn't wait to see what happened next.

ABOUT THE AUTHOR

With over 40 captivating titles spanning various genres, Quinn Avery honed her talent for crafting intricate puzzles through her smart and quirky Bexley Squires mystery series. Her contemporary suspense thrillers, often set in her beloved locales such as Lake Shetek and Mankato, Minnesota, are nothing short of addictive, leaving readers spellbound with their mind-spinning twists.

For more information, and a free ebook, visit www.QuinnAvery.com.

ACKNOWLEDGMENTS

To Najla Qamber: I love how the series covers all look together! Can't wait to get started on the next one!

To Jenny Hanson: Thanks yet AGAIN for loaning me your eagle eyes, and for being a loyal fan all these years!

To my editor, Jodi Henley: Thanks for hanging in there with this one even though it took forever! I always value your guidance and expertise!

To Corrie Hanson: Thanks for always having my back, no matter the situation! You've been an amazing friend throughout my journey!

To my super librarian friend, Heidi Schutt: Thank you for supporting my journey, and providing valuable feedback! Bago is lucky to have you!

To the local businesses, libraries, bloggers, and lovely people on Instagram who have helped to promote my work: I'm thankful beyond words! Thanks for taking a chance on me!

To my writer friends (notably Tracy, Micki, Kristie, Sierra, Leesa, Diana, Pam, Mira, Aubrey): Thank for you always being there. I love you all to pieces, and thank my lucky stars for having such talented friends!

To my "regular" friends who are anything BUT regular, and who have supported my career over the years (notably April, Denise, Michelle, Tara, Lori, Amy, Laura, Janet, Jess, Teresa, Misty, Krista, Cindy, Carolyn, and "crazy" Michelle): I wish I could buy you all a fabulous vacation for putting up with me, and being there at my signings! I have so much love for you all! 🤍

To my mom and dad: Thanks for being so supportive of my career!

To my husband and children: I know putting up with me while writing this one was especially brutal. Sorry.🤍

To my fans, new and old: THANK YOU from the bottom of my heart for following Bexley's adventures! Can't wait to bring you more of her in 2020!